THE ORPHAN NEXT DOOR

A SINGLE DADDY NEXT DOOR ROMANCE

ALISHA STAR

HOT AND STEAMY ROMANCE

CONTENTS

Blurb   v

1. Emily   1
2. Grant   6
3. Emily   16
4. Emily   22
5. Grant   29
6. Emily   42
7. Emily   48
8. Emily   55
9. Grant   61
    Sign Up to Receive Free Books   69
    Preview of The Virgin's Teacher   71
    Chapter One   74
    Chapter Two   78
    Chapter Three   86
    Chapter Four   90
    Chapter Five   98
    Chapter Six   103
    Chapter Seven   111

Other Books By This Author   125
Copyright   127

Made in "The United States" by:

Alisha Star

© Copyright 2020 – Alisha Star

ISBN: 978-1-64808-055-5

ALL RIGHTS RESERVED. No part of this publication may be reproduced or transmitted in any form whatsoever, electronic, or mechanical, including photocopying, recording, or by any informational storage or retrieval system without express written, dated and signed permission from the author

❀ Created with Vellum

BLURB

Emily is too young for me, but I can't shake how much I want her. I want to rescue her from her isolation. I certainly want to rescue her from that gold-digging little creep James.

I want to love her and be loved by her, and wake up to her face every morning. And of course, I'd love to make her mine. Even if our age difference didn't make me hesitate, James is doing his best to get and stay in the way, even after Emily throws him out of her life. He's stalking her; he's stalking us. And he's way too interested in my little girl for comfort. I'm determined to have Emily in my arms, safe from him and from the world's other predators. And when I finally get what I want, it's paradise. For a while, I don't think twice about that little brat and his complaining. But James isn't done. And as Emily and I work toward our first of what we hope is many Christmases to come, he's going to take his revenge. *I'm a patient man. But when he endangers my lover and my little girl, it is time for a reckoning.*

After living a life of extreme poverty, knowing nothing but neglect and loneliness, young Emily Dawn has won the New

York State Lottery and become a multi-millionaire. Having moved into the most modest house she can find in Woodstock, New York, she quickly develops a crush on her next door neighbor: self-made billionaire and single dad Grant Norton. They become fast friends, especially when his cute daughter, Molly, takes a liking to Emily.

But Emily has a problem. She's been dating the charming James Parrish: a handsome and age-appropriate young man from the neighborhood who's doing his best to seduce her and make her fall in love. Grant senses that something is wrong with the smarmy young man, but doesn't know if it's just his jealousy getting the better of him—as much as he tries to fight it, he can't help his attraction to the kind-hearted Emily. Determined to break Parrish's spell on her, Grant steps in—and the attraction between them ends up catching fire.

As their affair intensifies, they must figure out how to tell Grant's daughter, especially when Parrish starts to harass all three of them. Bent on revenge, the thwarted con artist finally resorts to trying to kidnap Molly. The lovers must join forces against him to protect the young girl, and sort out what is going on between them.

1

EMILY

As I stare out the window of my new mansion as a handsome man kisses my neck, the only thought in my head is that I wish he would stop distracting me. The thought shocks me as soon as it crosses my mind—James Parrish is beautiful, blond, and dashing—but it's true. There's something about his hands on me, his lips pressing softly and wetly on my pulse, which leaves me feeling soiled—like he's leaving behind some sticky residue wherever he touches.

He's trying harder than usual to be seductive, but after everything that's happened it's all I can do not to flinch away.

I have to hide my discomfort. Last time I begged off from having sex with him he demanded to know what was wrong with me. All normal girls want to fuck him once he puts the moves on them, or so he claimed.

I had to tell him that it must be the trauma from being on the streets, and the fact that I'm not used to being touched. But afterward I felt so much worse about myself that I've since made sure to never let on that I don't want him again. It's ridiculous that I have to work so hard to spare his feelings when we've only been together for a little while—and when he's never spared mine.

So I continue to let him kiss me and play with my tits through my sweater while I distract myself. I stare out past the drops of rain clinging to the glass and down the long, grassy hillside to my neighbor's back yard. Grant Norton is out there in the rain letting his two Golden Retrievers, Pogo and Mike, run. I smile to see him, a warmth running through me that James can't evoke any more.

The trick works; James chuckles, thinking my smile is meant for him, and pulls me closer, nuzzling my cheek as I hold him limply in my arms. He thinks I'm a slow starter when it comes to romance—and I am, having no real experience with sex or affection. But if I stay cold and still and don't smile, he'll get insulted again and sulk, and kick up drama.

So I look at Grant to get my heart racing—and since I can't have him, I turn around and settle for James.

"Aw, come on, Red, what's so interesting out there?" he wheedles, tugging at one of my strawberry blonde curls.

I look back at him and smile. "Everything."

It's true. After a life filled with institutional halls and filthy alleyways, my house in Woodstock is paradise. Looking out the window at all that green, gold, and crimson would soothe my soul even if Grant wasn't out there.

I drink him in with my gaze as I lie across the bottle-green velvet couch that dominates my living room. His tall, broad-shouldered form stands under a black umbrella as he tosses neon orange squeaky balls up the slope so the dogs can race after them. His dark hair ripples in the breeze along with his black overcoat; his strong face is a tanned blur at this distance, but I can picture his strong features in my mind.

Grant is the best part of living in Woodstock—besides being able to afford it, that is. After spending a chilly spring on the streets of Brooklyn, an amazing stroke of luck six months ago changed everything in my life. Now, I have a big house in the woods, a hot neighbor, a fridge full of food and a life to look forward to...once I recover from what I went through before it took a turn for the better.

Grant—watching him in his yard, talking to him, having lunch with him and his adorable daughter Molly—makes me happy to get up in the morning. His existence in my life reminds me of all I now have to be grateful for—and all I still wish I could have. His pale green eyes, so startling against his tanned skin, are full of kindness, and his smile is contagious. A few minutes of conversation with him helps my mood no matter how bad things get.

"Hey, are you listening, baby?" James whines, and I look back up into his blank blue eyes and force a smile.

"I'm sorry, I didn't really sleep. What did you say?"

He rolls his eyes, the corner of his mouth turning up. James is almost ethereally beautiful, with smooth skin and the face of a marble angel. I used to find that babyish look cute, but I'm starting to get tired of it—along with his whiny tone when he wants something. "I said, baby, order us up some pizza! I'm getting the munchies, and I know you haven't eaten all day."

He's right about that last part. I'm still getting used to the idea that I can fill my belly whenever I want, and have a bad habit of neglecting that need. It's almost as disorienting as looking at my account statements and wondering at all those zeros. It all still seems so...foreign...to be able to satisfy my hunger whenever I need to.

"Okay, okay." I dig in my pocket to see what cash I have: none. I usually don't carry much cash around. It's an old habit too, but this one's too smart to leave behind. "I can make the order but I have no cash on me. Can you get the tip?"

It's a simple request—it's only five dollars. But the petulant look on his face deepens, making my heart sink immediately. "Oh, come on, baby, you know I'm broke until my app rolls out. It's just another few weeks. And I know you're good for it." He gives a charming smile, and my stomach clenches with the sudden urge to tell him to *go away for good*. I know I have more options in the romance department than James wants me to think.

But no matter how many options I may have, none of them are the one I want. None of them are Grant, who is a widower twice my age with a little daughter, and who, as far as I can tell, does not date. I've had a crush on him since I moved in here, well before James got in my face two months ago and refused to leave.

James tells me that he's crazy in love with me. He tells me that there's never been anyone like me before, and that he wants to spend the rest of his life with me. Then he comes over and plants himself on my couch for hours, pushing for sex, expecting to be fed, and always asking for money.

I don't know what love is supposed to feel like, exactly, but I'm pretty sure it's not meant to feel like this. I think it's supposed to be more like how I feel when I'm around Grant, or when I see him with his daughter. All warm inside—with no reservations.

Right now, there's a chill deepening in my womb as I sit up, using it as an excuse to pull away from him. "Fine," I sigh. "What kind of pizza do you want?"

"Hawaiian, you know what I like." He waves his beer at me like he's ordering from a servant, and I shake my head as I pull out my phone. Pineapple doesn't belong on pizza.

I order a medium chicken pesto with mushrooms and olives for myself and a medium Hawaiian for him. I have stocked the fridge with beer, though I barely touch the stuff myself. I'm kind of hoping he'll get whiskey dick tonight and leave me alone.

I know deep down that these are not the sort of things that a girl should be thinking about with her first official boyfriend. But even though I'm nineteen and he's in his twenties, James is definitely the less mature one in our relationship. He's very charming when he wants to be, but right now it's clear to me what he thinks. He thinks he's won me and that he doesn't have to put in any effort at all to keep me.

But is he wrong? *Why am I still putting up with this?*

I already know. I don't like thinking about it. Part of it is that horrible, empty ache of loneliness that will yawn inside of me like a canyon the moment he leaves. The other is a deeper worry, but one that has nagged at me more and more—*what if he won't leave when I tell him to?*

I place the pizza order and put the tip on my card along with everything else. By the time I look back outside again, Grant is gone.

"So, baby doll, how much time do we have to...play...before our food gets here?" James drapes his hand over my shoulder and reaches down to cup my breast through my pale pink sweater. He gives it a squeeze that he thinks is friendly, and while it doesn't hurt, I have to force myself not to squirm.

"Twenty minutes," I make up, knowing it's more like forty, and he grunts in disgust.

"That's too little time," he grumbles.

"Hey, you were the one who wanted pizza," I remind him, and he finally shrugs and nods.

"Okay, fine. I'll just fuck you twice later." He offers a sleazy grin, and it's all I can do to force an answering smile.

2

GRANT

"Is Emily coming over to trick or treat with us?" Molly wrinkles her nose as I dab on her grease paint. She decided to go as a cat burglar this year, which, to her nine-year-old mind means a fuzzy white and cream kitty outfit with a robber's mask across her eyes.

"I'm going to ask her, though I don't know if she's had time to come up with a costume. Hold still, sweetie, I'm trying to get your kitty nose straight." Her whiskers were hard enough. Molly is incredibly energetic; even channeling it into martial arts training hasn't cured her of the wiggles.

But squirminess won't stop me. I'm determined to do daddy-daughter costumes justice. And thus, I am going trick-or-treating with Molly as Macavity from *Old Possum's Book of Practical Cats,* one of her favorites.

It took some planning behind her back, but it turned out well, and Molly squealed when she saw it. A cosplayer friend made it for me. I'm dressed in a black Victorian evening suit, with a stripy orange tail hanging out between its coattails, a top hat with kitty ears, another robber mask, and white gloves. I drew the line at face paint.

Woodstock is tiny, its houses scattered; anyone who wants a real trick-or-treat haul in the eastern Catskills has to be willing to drive from town to town. That is more than fine with me—I love to drive, and I am hoping to take my sweet neighbor Emily with us.

Emily is beautiful and kind, but she has no one. She's modest and hard-working as well, and Molly loves her. As for me...I'm starting to as well. If it wasn't for our huge age difference, I would love to pursue more than friendship with her.

But that's not why I want to take her along tonight. It's a lot more complicated than that, actually. I want her with me because I'm trying to pry loose a giant, smarmy blond leech that has attached himself to her.

Emily is young and big-hearted, but clearly traumatized and new to having money and a place to stay. The new boyfriend, James somebody, has circled in on her like a shark smelling blood in the water. He's local and a little notorious—a slacker with half a job delivering bread on his bike three seasons and shoveling driveways one. Like a lot of the spoiled sons of rich Woodstock residents, he lives on other people's money, and only works so his mother doesn't know how much weed he's buying.

Woodstock is big on gossip, especially when there's dirt to sling around. James is the son of a Hollywood producer and his trophy wife—his rich dad stashes him here with his mom to keep them out of the spotlight. James, who lives with his mother (with whom he shares a forgettable last name) between girlfriends, looks to be trying to make himself into a trophy husband.

I hate gold diggers of either sex. It's one of the reasons I have never remarried. Molly deserves to have two parents, but at least my wealth allows me to stay at home for her—except when one of my businesses has an important meeting, of course. And now, thanks to Emily, I don't even have to worry about vetting a stranger to babysit Molly while I'm gone.

I wish I could shake my growing desire to keep her.

As easy as it would be to place the blame on anyone else, I can't say it's entirely Molly's fault that I started becoming attracted to my nineteen-year-old neighbor. She didn't mean to put the idea in my head when she told me I should marry Emily so she could stay and take care of both of us. She just likes Emily and wants to keep her too.

Molly does not remember her mother, and I'm very glad of that. When we separated, Alicia said that going through with giving me a daughter was what had ruined our relationship. I don't fully understand her reasoning, but she complained that having a baby made her feel "too old."

I urged her to get counseling. I suspect to this day that it was postpartum depression. She simply wasn't like that before—wasn't like that when I fell in love with her. But Alicia was stubborn, and too proud. She refused to acknowledge that she had a problem.

I still remember the night she broke down and started shouting at me while Molly wailed in her bassinet, still too tiny to have any idea what was going on. She hated me, she hated Molly, she hated being sore and having stretch marks, and she hated her life with us most of all. I demanded that she seek treatment before her behavior started endangering herself and our baby, and she just laughed at me.

I ended up doing all the caring for Molly while Alicia refused to bond with her. Three months later she simply...drifted out of our lives. I woke up, she was gone, her things were gone, and our joint account had been cleaned out.

I went a little crazy trying to find her; her family wasn't cooperative, and the private investigators I hired turned up nothing. I had a newborn and felt, at the beginning, that Molly needed her mother. But Alicia vanished for an entire year before resurfacing again—in an obituary.

Persistence and a few bribes had gotten me the full police and coroner's reports. Molly's mother, whom I had loved for half my adult life, had been found semi-nude on a beach in Majorca. She had died out on the beach that lovely night, of what may have been a deliberate overdose on uncut cocaine and medical-grade morphine.

Further investigation indicated that she had spent the year and our money jet-setting around Europe pursuing every pleasure she could get her hands on—unaccompanied by anyone regularly, and contacting no one from her old life. She had been hospitalized for two previous suicide attempts: one in London and one in Amsterdam.

I've always shielded Molly from the truth about her mother. She only knows that her mother is dead. Not that she abandoned us and destroyed herself. And certainly not that I half blame myself for not taking steps to get Alicia into inpatient treatment before she disappeared.

Since then I've left off dating, focusing on two things: raising my daughter, and getting my head back together after learning the truth about Alicia. I don't rattle easy, but that genuinely haunts me. I didn't want to go into a new relationship dragging a lot of baggage, so I haven't even thought about it until recently.

Then along came Emily. And now I think about it all the time. Seeing Emily bond with Molly in a way that Alicia never could makes it even harder not to imagine her as a permanent part of my life—of our lives.

But Woodstock loves gossip, and I know what would happen if I actually made Emily that kind of offer. The idea of a rich billionaire marrying a girl half his age, who also happens to be his babysitter, would be tasty gossip-fodder. I don't care what the local biddies think of me, but Emily and Molly would have to live with any fallout as well. To spare them, I've forced myself to avoid even the semblance of flirting.

But I do care for Emily, and I do really want her. She's a good person, and she deserves to have people around her who care about her. Instead, she's sticking with that leech James, who is taking advantage of her inexperience and loneliness.

It's the one thing about her that frustrates me, and I can't blame her for it. Her heart is too big, and she expects too little from others. Far less than I would give her if I had the chance.

I rarely want to punch a guy in the face on first meeting, but this James guy gets to me. I've had a close encounter with someone like him before. Just thinking of James pawing at Emily in public makes my back teeth ache.

Emily may not be mine, but someone has to look after her. That may mean stepping in where James is concerned, so I'm always watchful. I don't want to get in her business unless invited, but I'll chuck all decorum out the window if he hurts her.

I step back and look at Molly, whose cream stripes and little pink nose are all even now. "There we go. Go have a look." I point at the full-length mirror across the bright bathroom, and she hurries over to it and squeals.

I lose the fight against grinning. "So did I do good?"

"Definitely an A+ job, Daddy. Now are we gonna pick up Emily?" She rocks on her heels, and my smile fades. I'm a little worried that Emily's too caught up in James's web and will let him keep her home.

"Let me call her and find out when." I don't want to presume and end up putting both Emily and Molly at the center of a tense and awkward scene. I punch in Emily's number as we walk out of the bathroom toward the rambling Victorian mansion's giant living room.

Both our Goldens sprawl out on the couch. I spent two good

hours wearing them out by throwing balls and letting them run up and down the grassy slope that separates Emily's house from my own. Neither of them raises their head as we come in, but both start thumping their tails against the couch cushions. Molly goes over to pet them while I wait for Emily to pick up.

It takes three rings. As I wait, I feel my blood pressure going up as I imagine her with James, trying to answer the phone. James pulling the phone out of her hands and going back to whatever inept sex act he's imposing on her.

I have seen her discomfort at the way he paws at her in public. If there was ever a rosy glow of new love between them, he must have spoiled it quickly with all his ass-grabbing antics. My sister Catherine is still on permanent vacation in Majorca, recovering from the scars that her own version of James left her with. As for my brother—he's always been a version of James.

When Emily picks up finally, all the air whooshes out of me in relief. "Whoo. Hey. Uh, it's Grant. Molly wants to know if you'll come trick-or-treating with us."

"Oh...oh hi!" Her voice perks up at once, and suddenly I'm calm again, feeling a mix of warm fuzzies in my chest area and a tightening in my groin. "Um, well, I—" she starts, and I hear the sudden, worried hesitation in her voice. "I'd like to."

I hear rustling in the background—and then a door opens. "Who is it, babe?" says a young man's voice, and my eyes narrow in annoyance.

"My neighbor needs a hand taking his little girl trick or treating," she replies in a voice that sounds a touch too cheery. My smile goes lopsided at her small display of cunning. I never said anything about *needing* her help with Molly, but if anybody asks me I'll back her story in a second.

"What? Aw, come *on,* baby, you have a boyfriend now. You've gotta stay home and take care of me!" His deep voice wheedles like a kid's.

"Take care of you? You're a grown—" she sighs and I hear her stop to take a deep breath before going on. *Just go ahead and yell at him, honey, he deserves every bit of it.*

But she doesn't, instead answering him with frustrating patience. "Look, James. We already talked about this. You're going to your mom's tonight." She speaks slowly and carefully, as if to a child with a volatile temper, and my heart sinks.

"Fuck my mom. I want the—" he starts, laughing off her concerns, trying to sound charming. He's the kind of guy who is used to letting his pretty face get him what he wants, just like his mother. "She'll be drunk by three in the afternoon anyway, she'll pass out before the servants bring out dinner. It doesn't matter."

"James, I sat there and listened to you promise her," she urges, but he just laughs some more. I hear rustling again and a small sound of discomfort from her, and a hot flush of rage runs through me.

Let her go, you son of a bitch. I want to say it aloud, but yelling through a phone is pointless. Should I go up the hill and rescue her from Mr. Won't-Take-No-For-An-Answer's grubby paws? I hesitate, my fist clenched, wanting to do just that.

Then, a small hand tugs at my pant leg. I look down and see Molly gazing up at me solemnly. She holds her hand out for the phone. I shake my head, but she stamps her foot insistently. "I've got a plan, Dad."

I pause, wondering what my imp is up to, and then hand her the phone.

Molly listens for a moment, frowns tremendously, sticks her finger in her ear and yells *"I wanna talk to Emily right now!"*

The argument over the phone stops at once, and I'm suddenly grinning again. I should be telling her that's not an inside voice. I don't.

She smiles. "Hi Emily! We're dressed as kitties and we need you to come help us trick-or-treat. So tell your stupid boyfriend to go back to his mommy! You've got other friends and he's just being selfish!"

My grin fades and I stare. My daughter surprises me regularly these days, but this one's a big one. *How are you nine?*

On the other end of the phone, Emily is laughing, and I hear James go "aw shit" almost sheepishly. Cute plus angry can be a potent combination. "Duty calls, sweetie. We've already got plans for tomorrow anyway, and you're out of clothes."

"Now that wouldn't happen if you let me leave some stuff here," he complains, but she cuts him off gently.

"James, I haven't even gotten used to living indoors yet, give me time before I give up my privacy entirely, okay?" Her voice is tender and patient...and is the exact same voice she uses with my nine-year-old.

Unfortunately, James is less reasonable than even Molly at her angriest and most overtired. "Oh come on, don't be a coward. I love you! We should be together. All the time."

You mean, "Your money and I should be together all the time," you damned parasite. My back teeth are still grinding together, and I hold myself still as Molly hands me the phone. *Don't do it Emily* I mouth, but if he hears me he'll make even more trouble for her.

"You shouldn't call me names," she says quietly. It's something Molly says to mean kids on the playground, but in Emily's mouth it is grave and edged with tension. James starts to stammer an answer, but she simply raises the phone back to her ear. "I need to get changed. You're doing cats?"

"Uh...yes, cat burglars, actually."

She laughs a little. "That's cute. Pick me up in fifteen minutes?"

I give Molly a thumbs-up, and snort as she bounces in place. "Sounds good. See you then."

She hangs up, cutting off James in the middle of a protest,

and I tuck my phone away, chuckling. *James zero, Emily and people who actually care about her, one.*

"So when do we pick her up?" Molly asks, eyes bright with anticipation.

"We leave in ten minutes," I announce cheerfully.

"Yay!" She hugs me around my waist, and we sit down on the couch to pet the dogs as we wait.

Twelve minutes later, we pull up to the curb outside Emily's house. It's one of the other huge old Victorians dotting the woods around Woodstock. She's having the old house refurbished bit by bit while she lives in it. They're not going to finish by winter, but all rooms are livable, and some are already gorgeously restored.

She told me once that the house was like her; falling apart in some places, but becoming new and lively again. No wonder James keeps trying to move in there, while she struggles to keep him out.

When I first found out that a New York State Lottery winner was moving in next door, I expected some brash, newly rich kid. Someone a little bit like James. Instead I got Emily—endlessly grateful for every bit of her new life.

She's told me only a little of the nightmares she's gone through, but I can see a lot of it in her eyes still. She has the haunted expression of someone who's spent most of her life so isolated and starved for love that even crappy, fake, fast-food romance like the kind James is offering feels good to her.

The door bangs open seconds after I pull up, and I see James come stomping out. He doesn't seem to notice my white SUV, which has darkened windows. Hands shoved deep in his pockets, he turns the corner and walks quickly down the street, shoulders hunched against the deepening cold.

I watch him, fighting the urge to laugh at him as he retreats back to his mother's house where he belongs. He disappears around the corner at the end of the street, and I sigh with relief. *Well, that's one problem out of the way. Temporarily, anyway.*

Then the door opens again, and I look up, my heart lifting. Emily comes out, her strawberry blonde curls shining in the dying sunlight, a pink puffy overcoat not quite concealing her slim curves. She's not in costume, but as her soft sea-blue eyes settle on my SUV and light up, I see she has a sparkly-tipped cat teaser toy in her hand.

3

EMILY

I know I shouldn't let myself feel guilty about leaving James behind to fend for himself this Halloween. It's not my fault he changed his plans the moment he discovered I had some that didn't involve him. If I ever do anything he dislikes, he makes it seem like I've committed a crime against him.

When we first got together, I was so starved for love that I was desperate to please James. Any dissatisfaction he showed was my signal to scramble to make things better so he would stay, so he would still love me. But soon, I noticed that all that attention, work, and support I was giving went only one way. He never gave anything back.

I've started getting stomach aches whenever I think of James. He is still beautiful, he can still coax a smile from me, and he has tons of friends around town that he promises to one day introduce me to. But after months together, I keep looking at what he says he'll do, and what he actually does, and I'm finally seeing the huge differences between the two.

The problem is, the man I really want is too good for me. But right now, sitting next to him in his car as we drive around Ulster

County looking for houses with welcoming lights, I can pretend that's not true. I can pretend that this is my family.

"All right, Daddy, don't forget to turn up the road ahead. If we don't get the big house at the top of the hill you won't get your booze cordials!" Molly is using a pen light to peer at a makeshift trick or treating map on the clipboard in front of her.

Grant chuckles. "Wouldn't want that." He sounds just a touch embarrassed, and I smile in the safe, warm dimness of the seat beside him.

James doesn't understand that there's a difference between someone who has never been loved and one who has never loved. I might scramble after affection like a starving dog, but that doesn't mean I'm not wary of being poisoned. In the end, like the dog, I have to make a choice: take the risk, or spend another night hungry.

Without Grant around, I might have been desperate enough to cling to James. But right now, when no one is making demands on me aside from company and a bit of babysitting and car-watching, I have something to hang onto besides him. Not just Grant, but the very idea of family, of closeness, of spending time out with people you love—and of holidays that mean something.

I can't help but think back on all those desolate years in the group home, with not a single card on Christmas, and only dirty snow clinging to the windows and turkey loaf for dinner. I could never understand why nobody wanted me, but even foster parents would not take me. Instead I was stuck trying to live peacefully in a place where the rejects go to live.

But instead of being a violent kid, or disabled, or too defiant to survive anywhere like a lot of the other kids at the home, I was just...shy and ordinary. I meant no harm to anyone. Yet even the craziest bullies left me alone once they found out about my past—found out that I used to be called Ebony Christchurch.

As horrible as it is, I actually wish I had known about my parents' lurid murder-suicide before I grew up. That whole time, I had no idea why nobody wanted to adopt or even foster me. Now I know they were just afraid I would turn out like John and Ellen Christchurch—the biological parents I can't remember.

One of the things I like most about Grant is that he knows, but he doesn't care. He's told me more than once that it doesn't matter who my parents were; it only matters who I am. I have always tried to be kind, gentle, thoughtful—not like my father. And not a worm, like my mother, either.

"So, what's the haul look like so far?" I ask Molly cheerfully, forcing my attention away from thoughts of my past.

"Two and a half bags, including four full-sized Snickers!" Molly declares proudly, and I hear Grant chuckle beside me. "Definitely an improvement from last year, except that Mrs. Exeter is now doing fun-sized M&Ms, down from full-sized last year. Gonna have to downgrade her house." From her tone, she believes this to be a real pity. Then she flips back a few pages on her clipboard and actually marks a checklist.

It's all I can do not to giggle when Molly gets going. She's precocious, smart, cute, and sometimes a bit of a pain in the butt—but she's nine after all, and it's never that big of a problem. Grant has done a good job with her.

Sometimes, when Molly begs me to stay longer, I wonder if she wouldn't do even better with a mother figure around. *But I'm not her mom, I'm her babysitter. I've never had a mom myself, how could I possibly know how to be one anyway?*

"You're very quiet," Grant says speculatively as we pull up at the next house. It's James's mom's mini-mansion near the hilltop. My throat tightens.

"That's James's house," I start, and then go quiet as I realize I have no idea at all how to explain why I don't want us going near it. "I'm not sure his mother is giving out candy."

"Might as well try!" Molly chirps, and opens the door, bounding out before Grant can follow.

"Hey, hey hold up!" He looks back at me. "Stay in the car where it's warm, I'll take care of this."

I nod and he shuts the door, shutting out the chilly air. I sit back against the cushioned seat, sighing out all my air, and watch through the tinted window as he trots after his speedy daughter.

She's knocking before he's halfway up the walk, and the door opens. James's tall, blonde mother, face so taut with plastic surgery that it looks stretched over a frame, appears with a pumpkin-colored bowl of candy. She smiles down at Molly—and then something happens that startles me so badly I don't know how to react.

James pushes the door wide open and all but shoves his mother out of the way as he grabs the candy bowl. He crouches down to address Molly, with a strangely determined look on his face. And he starts asking her questions.

I can't tell what he's asking exactly, but between his expression and the quick way she takes a step back from him, I'm suspecting it's pretty aggressive. His mother puts a hand on his shoulder and pleads half-audibly. He shrugs her off and keeps hammering Molly with questions as she backs up another step.

Oh fuck. She's a kid—what the hell is he doing? Horrified, I reach for the door—but Grant gets there before I can step outside.

James looks up as Grant says something and his eyes widen. He scuttles backwards through the door as if Grant took a swing at him. Molly points at him and laughs. His mother shoves him out of sight and comes forward with the candy bowl and an apologetic look.

I sit back in the seat and close my eyes, sick to my stomach. My face is burning; being associated with James in any way mortifies me right now, and I don't even know what he's said. *Oh God, what did he do?*

As they return to the car, James's mom stands at her door with her hands over her face. Molly is still giggling and Grant is seething. For a moment, used to being the scapegoat, I expect him to start yelling at me. Instead, as Molly snickers and buckles her seatbelt, he sighs.

"I should have listened when you tried to warn us about this house. Has James been jealous this whole time?" He's speaking in as calm a voice as he can manage, but I hear the edge to it that his giggling daughter misses.

"Jealous?" *Oh no. Not this again.* "He's jealous of everyone I spend time with who isn't him, if that is what you mean."

"Not that kind of jealous." He turns a tight smile on me. "He just interrogated Molly about the nature of our relationship."

My heart pounds even harder. I'm blushing so hard it hurts. Am I allowed to hate James for this, when he's the only one who has ever loved me to any degree?

"I'm sorry. I should have been more clear."

"Don't be sorry. It's just that times like this make me wonder why you're with him." He sounds far more worried than annoyed, and I have to fight back tears.

"It's times like this that make me wonder why I am, too." Admitting it eases some of my confusion.

"We should talk about this. But not right now." He touches my arm, and my lips tremble as I squeeze my eyes shut.

Molly snorts as she goes back to sorting her loot. "He's dumb. He kept asking me the same question over and over. I don't think he listens too well."

"No, he doesn't," I admit slowly. "Really, he seems a little...out of it sometimes." It's all the pot and cheap alcohol, mixed with the crazy hours he keeps. I'm almost sure of it.

Molly giggles again. "He wanted to know if you were sleeping with Daddy."

My mouth closes suddenly. *Oh God.*

Grant nods, his jaw set. "That's not the word he used, either."

I go very cold inside. "What did he say?"

4

EMILY

"You repeatedly asked my neighbor's nine-year-old daughter if I was fucking him? Are you completely crazy?"

WE'RE ON MY NARROW, covered front porch. I've shut the door behind me to keep the heat in—and James out. I'm in my fluffy rose-colored robe over a flannel nightie, and the icy wind cuts through both.

MY VOICE ECHOES down the street and off the hills. Two doors down, one of my neighbors turns off his music to listen. I don't care.

I'M NOT GOING INSIDE until James is well away from the porch. He's not coming in tonight. If he keeps this up, he's not coming in any night.

"Calm down, baby," James replies casually with a little smirk on his face, as if he's amused by how upset I am. "That can't be the first time she's heard the word 'fucking' before." He uncurls his hand and shrugs a shoulder. "The little slut's nine, not five."

HE CALLED MOLLY A—!

HE RAMBLES ON, oblivious to my reaction and smirking with his eyes half-closed from all the pot, while I turn to ice and stone inside. I can't even understand the noises coming out of his annoying mouth any more, and when I walk toward him he doesn't seem to notice. I don't know what I'm going to do until my palm slams against the side of his face hard enough that it goes numb.

HE LETS out a squawk as he loses his balance on the railing, his once casual stance turning to flailing as he launches off the short stairway. He lands on his ass on the walkway below with his smirk crumbling into a confused look.

SOMEWHERE DOWN THE street I hear howls of laughter. I ignore the laughing and walk slowly down the stairs toward James, all hell and fury in a pink fluffy robe.

HE BLINKS AND LOOKS AROUND, as if trying to figure out if he tripped, and then the blood returns to his cheek and he claps a hand over it. "Ow!"

. . .

I stand over him while the wind plays with my hair, my whole body feeling like it's burning inside. "Don't you ever talk about that little girl that way again."

His eyes widen as it dawns on him what the hell just happened, and he fixes me with an astonished look. He outweighs me by half, and I'm usually all that is timid and retiring, but suddenly he's on the ground and my tiny ass is hovering menacingly over him. I wonder if he thinks he's gone crazy.

Finally, he stammers, "You...you fucking slapped me!"

"Yeah, I did. And there's more where that came from." I move closer to him, and he actually scoots back away from me as I approach. *Good.* "You do not call any girl a little slut, let alone one who is a literal child. If you *ever* say or do anything inappropriate to or about Molly or any other child in this town, I will track you down. I will beat your ass, and then drag what's left of you down the hill to the police station." My fists clench and my voice trembles, and it takes everything I have not to bend down and hit him again.

All he is doing is staring at me, blinking. He isn't making a single bit of effort to get up. "Are you on bath salts?" he finally mumbles.

I guess he never realized the volcano of anger I've been fighting down inside me for so many years. He seems terrified of it now, and is still trying to rationalize my rage.

· · ·

I LAUGH BITTERLY. "Whatever gets you off my lawn and out of my life, you can feel free to believe. But you really fucked up tonight, and since you can't even figure that out, it's time for you to go."

I IGNORE the deep panic welling inside of me and just point down the walk. "Let your mother deal with your creepy ass from now on. I'm done."

"YOU'RE BREAKING UP WITH ME?" That finally gets him to his feet. His smile wavers back onto his face and he lets out an incredulous laugh. "You're kidding me. Over a kid?"

"No, not over a kid. Over your being so fucking inappropriate with the little girl that I babysit that I will never allow you around her again. And God help you when her father finds out about this!" I take a step towards him. He smirks and stands his ground...and when I don't hesitate, he scuttles back like he did from Grant earlier.

"LOOK, OKAY, I GET IT," he says as he backs up with his hands spread in front of him. "You're obviously upset about something. You're not explaining it well because you're upset, and I don't know, maybe you're premenstrual."

I GLARE AT HIM, and his smile crumbles the rest of the way. "I'll come by tomorrow and see if you're feeling better," he mumbles in a rush, and turns to hurry off down the street.

. . .

"Don't bother!" I call after him, but inside my guts are already curdling as I feel the connection between us start to fray. Loneliness yawns like a chasm in my future, and for a split second a wave of terror overwhelms my anger.

There will never be anyone once this one is gone, whispers the fear in the back of my head. The cold starts seeping into my bones and I almost slip as I hurry back inside and lock the door, tears already streaming down my face.

I can't get warm even though I know the heat is on full blast. I huddle in my gown and robe on my couch and feel the chill like a patch of ice deep inside me.

But despite my panic, and despite my pain, I don't call James. He's spent months making me realize that sometimes the loneliness I fear is safer than being with the wrong person. And James isn't just wrong for me—he's wrong for the other people in my life, few though they may be.

If he was just a danger to me, or to my wallet, that would be one thing. But he showed no consideration for that poor child, and didn't even seem to be aware that he was doing anything wrong. *Or maybe he just doesn't care.*

One of the things I learned during all those lonely nights of my childhood was to force myself to stop dwelling on how unfair it was I had no one to care for me. Self-pity has only ever brought me down.

But right now, it is so hard not to fall into a depression that I feel like I'm being haunted. Every room in my huge house yawns around me like the vacuum of space, deepening the chill inside of me.

In my mind I'm not here, safe in my home any more.

I'm on the street, sleeping beside a dumpster now that I've aged out of the group home I grew up in, scratching bedbug bites that leave scars on my skin for almost a year. I'm starving, having lost twenty pounds in two months—not a pound of which I can spare. I'm outside with another group of street kids, nearly getting stabbed over a dry refrigerator box in a rainstorm.

I'm sitting through Christmas morning on my bunk, watching a dozen other kids tear open gifts from distant relatives and charities. My hands are empty.

I'm in the library, reading old news articles on the computer as I linger there to stay warm, and coming across the story about my parents, and how they died.

Then my phone is ringing in the pocket of my robe, and I'm back in the present again, heart pounding as I pull it out.

"Hello?" I mumble, my lips still numb. The feelings from my past recede enough that I can think and talk, even with my face streaked with tears.

"Hi there." Not James—*thank God*—but Grant, sounding concerned. "I heard yelling. Are you all right?"

My throat tightens and I squeeze my eyelids shut. I don't want his pity. I don't want to look like a basket case. I don't want to scare him off by seeming needy—I can't risk having one of the only people I actually feel good being around walk out of my life right after James.

"Emily. Sweetheart." His voice chides me very gently, and I shiver and swallow hard. "No lies now. Do you need me to come over?"

I sniffle, and then start sobbing quietly. "Yes," I finally admit.
"I'm on my way."

5

GRANT

I can't leave my little girl alone, any more than I can leave Emily alone, so I go to Emily's to pick her up and bring her back to my home. The moment I walk into her house and see the lost look in her eyes, I know I'm doing the right thing. Within five minutes, I'm ushering her in my door, having wrapped her in a down coat over her robe and helped her into proper shoes.

"Molly's sleeping," I warn in a hushed voice as I shut the door behind us. She swallows and nods, and I lead her into the house and take her coat. My house is a bit smaller than hers, but it's fully decorated, mostly in warm wood tones, cream, and touches of blue. The dogs have woken up and come padding down the stairs to greet us, feathery gold tails wagging hard as they see Emily.

"Hi guys," she says in a weepy voice as she crouches down to hug them and get some doggie kisses. She's breathing raggedly, fighting a fit of tears with all her remaining strength. I don't know exactly what's wrong, but I can guess that it has to do with James's supremely creepy antics earlier.

I got in earshot of him within a few seconds of seeing that little creep crouch down to confront Molly. Just that one same question, over and over again. "Hi honey. If you want candy, I gotta get you to answer something...Is he fucking her? No, no, tell me first, then candy. That's the deal. Is. He. Fucking. Her?"

It was all I could do not to lay him out at his mother's feet with one punch for exposing Molly to that. And now, it seemed, I have to clean up the rest of his mess.

At least it is Emily that needs caring for. That is hardly a chore. As I lead her over to the couch with the dogs trailing after, I can feel her shaking. I do my best to keep calm and keep my voice low as I help her sit down, and then sit down beside her.

"Can I get you anything, sweetheart?" I ask, covering one of her hands with my own. The dogs flop down at our feet and watch us, both doing the worried eyebrow-wiggle dogs do when they sense tension.

She smiles sadly. "In a little. Right now I probably won't be able to keep anything down."

"Emily, this isn't good. This guy..." I hesitate, seeing her lips start to tremble. "Okay, look. How about you talk, and I listen?" I drag a box of tissues closer.

HER SMILE IS thin and wobbly, ready to go away with the slightest hint of additional pain. But I'm not giving it to her. It's why I'm not sitting there bitching about the asshole who has latched onto her. Pressuring her to kick James to the curb wouldn't work anyway; too easy for her to view it as criticism of her for being victimized.

"I CONFRONTED him about what he did to Molly when he tried to come over. He wasn't even supposed to come over that late. But he didn't care. He started complaining about his mom "smothering" him, but I know he basically wanted a booty call." The corner of her mouth tugs up a little bit, as if she's taking bitter satisfaction in what happened next.

I SMILE AT HER ENCOURAGINGLY. "So you gave him hell, huh? Thanks for that. I'm afraid if I did it he'd end up in the hospital and me behind bars. I'm not lying when I say that the guy deserves it."

"YOU'RE PROBABLY RIGHT...HE tried to say that it was fine to talk like that to a nine-year-old. Then he insulted her and I..." She trails off, going from pale to red and then back again. "Sort of...might have...committed assault against him."

I STARE. "YOU PUNCHED HIM?"

. . .

"Slapped." She's red again, but fighting down a tiny, naughty, maybe even proud smile. "I um...knocked him off the porch. He didn't want to come too close to me after that."

Holy shit. She should have dressed as Wonder Woman tonight. I blink at her several times, not sure what to say—and then I have to stifle a laugh behind my hand before I wake up Molly. "You're kidding me!"

"Um, no, not at all. He actually was very surprised. But he wouldn't stop no matter what I told him, and he wanted to get into my house when I had already decided not to let him in tonight." She runs a hand back through her tangled curls, which have all but escaped her ponytail.

"Is this his usual kind of behavior? I thought that you were pretty serious with him." I can't keep the concern out of my voice.

"He's never been this bad. I think that for a while he was on his best behavior until he could take a guess at how much bullshit I would put up with. But he was wrong." She wipes a tear away with her fingers and I hand her the Kleenex box.

"You seem pretty upset for someone who just dropped about a hundred and seventy pounds of dead weight, honey." I can't help but move closer and slip an arm around her. She shivers, and for a moment I hesitate and almost pull away—but then she moves closer and throws an arm around my chest.

It takes everything I have to ignore my body's immediate response to her warm softness pressed against me. I haven't had a lover in over six months, and I'm suddenly remembering how much I miss it. I force myself to just sit there, enjoying her sweet smell and her shining hair spilling onto my shoulder as she lays her cheek against me.

"He's the only one who's ever loved me," she mumbles, and I go cold.

I hesitate. If I say "that wasn't love" it could throw her deeper into despair. I could confess my own feelings for her, and hope that she trusts it. I have to step carefully, because as loving and thoughtful as Emily is, she is also inexperienced as hell—and scarred.

She's confided some about her lack of a family—and I've done the research on her biological parents. The newspaper articles, the morgue reports on her father's victims, the murder-suicide. I have always hoped that maybe she hasn't actually read all those things, but I know it's a vain hope. It's her personal history, after all.

"Sweetheart, I'm sorry, but you're wrong," I say finally, reaching over to stroke her hair as she clings to me. "He's not the only person to love you. He's just the first person, and he isn't very good at it. He doesn't treat you well, or the people you care about. And anyone who can't be trusted around a kid probably can't be trusted with your heart or body either."

She presses her lips together and those sea-blue eyes get bright again, and I just want to cuddle her until this all goes away. But I can't, can I? I'm too old for her.

"You don't see me as a kid?" she asks softly.

"Huh? Oh. No, no, I don't. I never have. You're younger than me, but you're far from a child. Have I...treated you like you are?" My cock is throbbing inside of my jeans, pushing at the fabric, as her heartbeat picks up against my chest.

She thinks about it a moment. "I don't have much experience," she admits quietly. "Not with people treating me like I'm...not just grown, but...acceptable."

A sudden, ugly suspicion fills my head, and she looks at me in alarm as I tense up. "It's okay," I mumble, and start stroking her hair again. "I just need to ask you some things about James."

If it turns out that that bastard has been playing on her insecurities to get his way, I may just beat the hell out of him, grieving mother or no grieving mother. I don't even care if she sues me.

She raises her head from my shoulder, her eyes bleary and confused. "What is it?"

"Does James know about your past?" I ask her softly. I'm praying that I'm wrong about all this, and he's just another dumb, horny kid with no self-discipline or social skills.

"I...told him I was an orphan and grew up in a group home. He knows I'm here because I won the lottery and that I was on the streets for a while before that." She still sounds confused. "Why?"

"Did you tell him anything about your real name or your parents? Like you told me?" I am keeping my tone as gentle as possible. I can't just tell her that this prick is bad for her and expect it to stick, or expect her to feel strong and supported enough to act on it.

I can already tell that James isn't going to let this lie. Not after today's drama. He's a dumb, arrogant kid with an attitude problem—he won't know when to let something like this go.

More than that, he's a parasite, and he'll be reluctant to give up someone he's using. He was spoiled as a kid and learned to bank on his looks and manipulation to get everything he ever wanted. He won't believe for a second that, slap or no slap, Emily actually meant it when she dumped him tonight.

HER COPPERY BROWS DRAW TOGETHER. "No, I didn't. I mean, I almost told him my old name, since I don't think he even knows how to do a Google search. But I never told him that part of my life. Not one bit of it."

A HUGE WAVE of relief runs through me. To someone like James, a secret like Emily's murderous parents would only be ammunition. If he ever finds out the whole story, I know it will be all over Woodstock in a matter of days…and poor Emily will suffer because of it. "So you trusted me with that information, but not him? Why?"

AGAIN, that puzzled look—as if she hasn't given much thought to it before. "Instinct," she says quietly. "That and…I'm taking care of your kid. If you found out I was hiding something like that, you might not trust me anymore."

I GIVE HER A SUPPORTIVE SMILE. "I want to think that I would understand better than you think, sweetheart, but that wasn't my point." I rub my chin. "Let me put this another way then. Would you ever trust James with that information?"

"No," she says immediately, and then pauses. I can see her mind chewing all this over, and she doesn't seem very happy with the conclusion she's drawing. "He's used the homeless and orphan part against me in arguments and when he's wanted something. Telling him my parents went on a killing spree and then finished each other off before the police could catch them would...he..."

Her eyes widen, and even though I feel bad I have to put her through this turmoil to bring her to these realizations, most of what I feel is relief. She's getting there.

"Look, sweetheart, I know it's your life, and I admit I have some ulterior motives, but the bottom line is, I care about you. I don't want to see you hurt by this guy or anyone else." We're cuddling again, and her eyes are dry now as she gazes up at me. She has relaxed a little bit.

"I told him to go away," she murmurs, and I nod at her. "But...is that...good enough?"

"No, no. I'm sorry, but chances are, no. Chances are, he's going to show up with flowers, or bud, or some gift that might actually be thoughtful, and he's going to try every day until he wins you back." I feel terrible telling her all this.

"So he's devoted...but only because he wants something from me. Money. Sex." She laughs sadly and has to reach for another tissue.

. . .

"I'm sorry, sweetheart. It's part of why I keep saying that you deserve better. Because you really, really do. You deserve to be with someone who will make you happy." *Someone like me.* It's on the tip of my damn tongue, but I can only imagine the emotional whiplash that would cause.

"How do you know so much about what James will do?" She doesn't sound suspicious—just surprised. "You don't seem like the kind of person who would end up treating a girl like that, even when you were James's age."

I've got about a decade on James, which of course is a lot of time for growing up, but something in her tone catches my attention. "How...old did James tell you he is?"

"Three years older than me. Twenty-two." She gives me a blank look as my heart sinks. "Why?"

"Sweetie, he's almost thirty." Her eyes widen in horror, and I sigh, suddenly wishing I had a joint. I don't keep any in the house with Molly around, though.

"What?"

My heart sinks at the horror in her tone. *She really doesn't like older guys,* I think with a mix of disappointment and self-disgust.

. . .

"Look, I know you have lived in Woodstock for a lot of years, but...I...." Her eyes track back and forth in shock and horror.

"Yeah, well, he's a local kid, and he's always pissing somebody off, so word gets around. He's a bad case of arrested development."

A very bad case. Always in denim and hoodies or skater wear, dressing like a teenager, acting like one, too. Working shitty low-level jobs because he has no focus. Hanging out with younger kids and pretending to be one, because he can't keep friends long and the new crop will think he's cool because he brings the weed.

Woodstock has always been full of people like James, male and female, never wanting to grow up or support themselves—or anyone else. I love my town, but it's got problems—and James is absolutely one of them.

"Oh God, how...I mean...how can someone get to be almost thirty and be that...childish?" she says in shocked disgust. "I understand him maybe being spoiled as a kid, and I know people my age don't always make the best decisions, but he's..."

She trails off, hands over her face, and I pet her hair and wait for her. Finally, she lifts her head, still looking a bit sniffly and red-eyed. "You never answered my question. How do you know so much about guys like James, anyway?"

. . .

I HESITATE. I don't want to bring up my idiot younger brother Evan unless I have to. Not yet. "I...I've seen guys like James before. I went to Yale with a ton of them. They don't have money of their own since they won't actually work, but they're really used to living lavishly off other people's money. So once their parents get sick of them, they latch onto someone else."

I GESTURE FOR A MOMENT, trying to come up with the best way of saying this. "You are new to being wealthy, you are very young, and you have very little social and romantic experience. You also tend to withdraw from people."

I SAY this as kindly as I can, but she still looks a little embarrassed and has to wipe her eyes again. "James is a predator and an opportunist. He probably thought you would be an easy target. I'm just really glad he was wrong."

"ME TOO." She takes a shivery breath. "Love shouldn't hurt this much. I don't know much about it, but I do know that much."

"NO, no, it never should. Something is wrong if it does." I wish I could have found her before James, so I could have helped her build up her sense of self-respect before he had a chance to pounce. I don't know if he conned her into sex yet, but I know he must have made a pest of himself trying.

. . .

"I'm...so glad I never said yes to him moving in," she murmured in breathless horror. "Maybe I should take a break from dating. I've even thought about just giving up and being that spinster lady with a million pets," she mumbles.

The amount of alarm I feel as she states this is almost ridiculous. "Uh, please don't do that. At least not the spinster part." I laugh awkwardly, and she blinks. I speak hastily. "Every unmarried man in the state of New York would be disappointed if you did that, including me."

Now she really is staring at me, because I really did just put my foot in it in a gigantic way. I just gave away everything. I feel like a horny, awkward idiot. She just broke up with someone. Even if I wasn't twice her age—!

She darts forward suddenly, and I feel her soft little lips caress my own. I freeze in place, absolutely astonished, and stare down at her, blinking. My whole body is thrumming with the urge to return the kiss...and do a whole lot more. But instead, I hold still, my arms still around her, but letting her call the play.

"I'll keep that in mind for when I'm over this mess," she says softly, and I feel my heart leap with relieved amazement.

6

EMILY

I'm sleeping in my bed, but somehow I'm also back in Grant's living room, curled in his arms with the dogs at our feet, kissing him. Everything is hazy and sweet, but underneath all that is my hunger to feel more of him. His mouth...his hands...his body.

What I feel for Grant is far more real than what I felt for James, because there's nothing forced or uncomfortable about it. James's attention lured my starving heart—lured me all the way into bed with him. It's not that I didn't feel any desire for him—he is handsome, and I did want him at first. But in spite of my initial desire for him, what happened after I joined him in bed killed my desire and left me frustrated and unfulfilled.

Not to mention sore, sticky, disgusted, and in need of a shower.

Love isn't supposed to be like that, Grant reassured me on that weepy night I broke up with James, and more than once in the week since. I believe him. And after his admission—and that kiss—I'm starting to understand what it might feel like, with the right man.

He's twice my age. People will talk. I don't know if I could ever be a good mom to Molly. But still, here I am on the couch with him again, for the third night this week.

We kiss like we're starved for each other, our hands working under each other's clothes, and I remember again that beautiful, delirious hunger I felt my first time—before James ruined everything. But this time it's far stronger, and far more pure—with no misgivings, no fear.

The lights go out. The feeling of his hands on me grows vague as my dreaming mind gropes for tender sensations...and finds no memory to pin these feelings on. Instead, we kiss and kiss endlessly, until I feel his weight sink down over me, and my desire and bliss grow so sharp and strong they wake me up.

I sit up, gasping in the dark with my whole body trembling, nipples painfully hard, cunt aching with so much need that it alarms me. The fact that it's a dream disappoints me deeply...but I know it's for the best. Grant is interested, and so am I...but I have healing to do.

"Grant and Molly have invited me to Thanksgiving and Christmas," I tell my financial advisor, Ora Northman, during our monthly check in a week and a half later. "It's my first time, um, celebrating."

Ora is in her forties and built like a fertility goddess, with long jet-black micro-braids, bronze skin, generous features and intense, dark eyes that stare at me shrewdly. "Emily, the more you tell me about that group home you grew up in, the more I think they were crazy to put you there. How does that place still have its license?"

"I don't know. Grant sometimes talks about suing them. But I'm wondering if exposing them wouldn't do more. I have enough money, now." I don't know what I would do if I had the kind of money Grant has—I can hardly figure out what to do with my millions, never mind a couple billion. I know he's invested heavily in many charity and community programs, and that he has a huge trust fund for Molly, but my eighteen million after taxes is more than enough for me.

Especially with Ora guiding me in how to manage it.

"That's an interesting idea, but you have to do it in a way that won't lead to them suing. Though provoking them to make the first move legally might actually be shrewd, if you're planning to see them in court anyway." She winks, and I fight a smile.

"Maybe. Right now I have some more immediate problems, and I...well..." I squirm in my plush velvet seat as I sit across the desk from her. The chairs are done up in rosewood and deep burgundy, and the velvet hisses slightly against the back of my forest green wool dress.

"Emily, you know I told you to come to me with anything. I know you're kind of short on friends right now, since you're out on your own for the first time. It hasn't been that long. I'm just glad to hear Grant and Molly are stepping up. Now, what's this about that boy James?"

"I broke up with him," I say, and she cracks a smile.

"Well it's about time! We'll have to celebrate." Her eyes twinkle, and I know what that means—sugar-loaded cappuccinos at the coffee shop on the corner. Her office in Poughkeepsie is home to a lot of cafes, being right near the college campus.

"Sounds good. Grant doesn't need me for Molly until late morning tomorrow, so I don't mind a late drive back." I'm proud of myself for getting so used to driving. I have gotten good at it with Grant and Ora's careful help.

"Good!" She checks the figures on her laptop. "Well, we're seeing the same kind of slow but steady growth on your mixed investments. Precious metals will be up all through this half of the year thanks to the holidays and end-of-year investments, so you'll see a bonus here. On a conservative estimate with your mixed portfolio, you'll be seeing roughly one million a year after taxes. How much that grows will depend on how much you reinvest."

I nod, struggling to follow along, as my head is still full of gossip about James and Grant. It's a staggering amount. I can't even imagine how I could spend a million a year. "Probably at least half of it."

"That's wise." She types a few notes as I sit there thinking.

And then it comes to me. The mess that James has left me with leaves my head altogether for one amazing moment of clarity. "I've got it."

"You've got what?" Ora raises an eyebrow and her hands drift toward her keyboard.

"Buy it."

She blinks once, and then both her eyebrows go up. "Buy Cranburg House? The group home where you grew up?"

"If I sue them that place will collapse completely, and the kids still stuck there will have nowhere to go through no fault of their own. If I buy the owner out, fire any of the staff who are part of the problem, and take over..."

Ora's face brightens "Now this sounds like an actual plan for your future besides 'recover from everything in my new house' like you've been doing so far." She leans forward, fingers steepling. "Tell me more."

By the time we leave for the coffee house, we have the basic outline of a plan to approach the absentee owner of Cranburg House about selling. We both order peppermint mochas with ridiculous amounts of whipped cream and a pair of cannolis that threaten both my outfit and my waistline, but at the moment, I barely care.

Even with the mess of my breakup, I have things to look forward to now. The gentle heat that's growing between me and Grant. My growing investments. My developing life goals. The list of good things coming my way keeps getting longer. And as for my past...well, it will be a great help knowing that the place that stole my childhood won't have a chance to do that to anyone else.

Maybe I really can handle this whole "adulting" thing after all, and maybe I'm more than just a lucky lottery winner. Maybe it will all be okay...if I can get rid of James for good.

"So, I know we didn't have time for it during your hour, but I was wondering what happened with your now ex-boyfriend. Have you seen him since you threw him out?" Ora slices the tip off one of the cannolis with the edge of her fork and scoops it into her mouth.

"Every single night around midnight, he gets drunk and tries to come by to 'make up.' The neighbors have called the cops on him twice." I sigh and take a sip of my drink, then wipe cream off the end of my nose.

"So you've never let him in?"

I shake my head. I have managed to stay strong, mostly because of Grant and Molly. Molly needs to be as far away from James as possible, just like me. As for Grant...unlike James, who half-assed everything, Grant's actions, his words—*that kiss*—all tell me that he is offering the real thing.

I am tired of living on emotional scraps. I want this. I don't want James. "No. Once I found out he's twenty-eight and has been scamming rich women for a decade, I was done."

"He's twenty-eight?" Her perfectly lined brows go up before crumpling in disgust. "Ew."

I suddenly find myself rushing to defend...something. "It's not his age. I would actually prefer someone more mature than me, but...James lied. He's also...less mature than me, by a lot."

"Yeah, I'm getting that impression. So what about this guy Grant? You're spending the holidays with him. I know he's a little old for you, but have you ever thought...?" Ora props her chin on her hand and gives me a thoughtful little half-smile. "I mean, it sounds like you're already becoming a part of his life."

I take a deep breath, and come out with it. Ora is very observant and doesn't like her intelligence being insulted. "I love him. And I know he likes me. He's even attracted to me. I just don't know..." I chew my lip, and then distract myself with a few bites of my cannoli.

"You don't know what, honey?" Ora sits back, an amused look in her eyes. "It sounds pretty straightforward to me. You love the guy, and he sounds good for you. As for James, well, his mom can take care of him, since she's the one who spoiled him."

A weight lifts off my heart at her words, but the apprehension behind it doesn't quite go away. "I haven't ever been in love before. What if I mess things up?"

She gazes at me with those shrewd eyes and I feel a little foolish, but she's still smiling. "Then you apologize, learn from it, and try again. Relationships don't usually die on one screw-up, honey, they die from people's refusal to grow and learn to do better by each other."

7

EMILY

I'm still thinking about Ora's advice as I pull into my driveway. I drove happily the whole way home. Under the bright moonlight and the glare from the highway lights, I listened to soundtracks from some of my favorite movies so lyrics didn't distract me from the road. My heart was full of optimism thanks to my time with Ora, and that feeling lasts up until the moment my headlights splash across James lounging against my garage door.

For a moment, I fantasize about hitting the gas instead of the brakes and sending him flying through the heavy wood door. I can afford a really good lawyer now, after all. But then I force myself to stop, and calm down as best I can. *I'm not like my father.*

Still, I'm good and angry when I finish locking my car and turn to go up the walk.

. . .

I walk right past James, ignoring him as he tries to talk to me, and only hesitate when I reach the edge of my porch. It's even colder than the night we broke up, my breath misting and a few flakes of snow drifting down.

"Hey," he calls after me, sounding shocked and outraged. His hand grabs my shoulder, and my skin crawls as I immediately struggle to shake him off. "Come on, Emily! You won't even talk to me!"

I spin around, breaking his grip, my eyes flashing. "Do not put your hands on me. You've lost that privilege for good."

His hands go up as his eyes widen. "Holy fuck, don't hit me again!"

I put my hands on my hips to keep them from going around his throat. "You are pushing thirty, James. Do not pull this scared little boy shit with me. And don't play stupid, either. You know why I have a problem with you right now. So get the hell off my land!"

I don't know how I keep my voice down, but apparently the look on my face is enough to unnerve him. But he still stupidly stands his ground. "This isn't fair, Emily. So I lied about my age and wasn't polite to some stupid kid you're babysitting. Fuck that brat and her dad, it's not like you need the paycheck!"

. . .

"Fear of consequences is not the only reason to be a decent person, James. But if that's the only thing that will work for you, then fine. I'll get a restraining order." Ora seconded Grant's opinion that I should get one, and after this, I'm sold.

"A restraining order?" The incredulous laugh in his voice makes me sick. "That's completely crazy, Emily! Come on, baby, don't be like this. Don't do this. I love you."

"No, you don't, okay? Stop it, James. You want my money, and my body. You don't want me. And you don't even need any of that, because if your mother will keep putting up with you after you accost a child right in front of her, she is *never* going to cut you loose." How am I keeping my voice so even?

"Wrong. Jesus, you are so wrong." The laugh in his voice sounds more nervous than mocking now. "Of course I want you. Your money and your booty are all just part of the package! And I like the package." He gives me a sleazy smile, and my stomach lurches.

"But you don't give a fuck about what's inside," I mumble. I turn to walk away—and he tries to grab me again.

Neither of us have raised our voices. Neither one of us has knocked anything over. Yet somehow, someone has noticed us.

I discover that Grant has let his dogs off their leash mid-walk when two big, barrel-chested streaks dart up the walk and skid to a stop right beside me. Pogo and Mike stand at each of my flanks, and one of them—Mike, I think—lets out a deep growl.

JAMES SKITTERS BACKWARD AGAIN, and I glare at him. "Look. You had several chances. You fucked up, you lied, and you keep doing both. You never learn. I cannot deal with that in my life. Go back to your mother and let her take care of you. I need to take care of myself."

HIS MOUTH WORKS, but he hears Grant's heavy tread coming fast through the dark, and looks down into the snarling faces of two very protective dogs. And finally, he backs off, shooting me a petulant glare.

"YOU KNOW, I get it. You're gonna be a bitch to me for a while because you like kids and I don't. That's fine. I'll find a way back in."

"HEY!" Grant shouts, his voice as growly as those of his dogs, and James darts off into the night like a scared boy half his age. There's a pause—and then, to my shock, Grant runs right past my gate and after James.

OH SHIT. Everything seizes up inside of me, and I worry for a moment that this is going to end very badly. Grabbing both dogs' leashes, I let them tug me to the end of the walk, but no further. "Heel!" Thank God they both agree.

. . .

I can't see the pair on the dim street beyond my front yard, but I can hear their hushed, harsh conversation. "Look, man, what is your problem?" James whines.

"Stop stalking that girl," comes Grant's cold reply. "Leave her alone. Do not bother her again, or I'll make sure you do a lot more than sit in the drunk tank until Mommy picks you up."

"What the fuck—hey, that's my girlfriend! We're just going through a rough patch." Mock indignation replaces James's wheedling tone. "It's none of your business."

"It is my business. She's my neighbor, my daughter's caretaker, and my friend. She dumped you weeks ago. Now lay off with this stalker crap and go home."

"Hey, fuck you, man! Her ass is mine! You're not moving in—" The sudden sound of a scuffle cuts off his voice for a few moments. "Ow! Man, what the fuck?"

"You're the idiot who accosted my daughter with inappropriate questions and then doubled down by calling her a 'little slut.' She is *nine*. I have already described the incident to the local cops. Believe me, they are watching your every move now, and if they don't get you...I will." There's so much danger and rage in Grant's voice that it even scares me. Yet somehow, most of what I feel is...gratitude.

. . .

"Look, I was drunk."

"That's no fucking excuse. Get out of here, and stay off this street."

I hear James's footsteps scrambling off down the damp sidewalk. My heart is beating so hard that I can't move. I realize that their conversation waded into violent territory, and it scares me.

Then Grant walks into sight and comes toward me with worry in his eyes. "You okay?"

I shake my head. "I'm so tired of this. I never know when he's going to pop up outside my house."

He takes me into his arms and hugs me tight, his down coat rustling under my cheek like a pillow. "I'm sorry, sweetheart. I'm glad I was outside when he started this. The cold makes voices carry."

I cling to him, closing my eyes. "I don't want to be alone tonight," I whisper.

He freezes for a moment, and then draws in a long, shuddering breath. Then he leans back to look down at me. "Okay then. Let's pack you a few things. You're staying at my place tonight, and in the morning I'll drive you to the police station to file that restraining order."

"Thank you," I mumble into his chest as the dogs mill around our legs.

8

EMILY

Grant insists on being a gentleman. He gets me and my clothes bundled into one of his guest rooms, has a drink with me, and tenderly kisses me goodnight. Then drives me up the wall by *leaving* and going down the hall to climb into his own bed.

Both dogs are in with Molly. I lie there in my bed in the cute, mint green silk nightie I packed, horny and hopeful, and wonder if I dare go down that hall as well. I lie there trying to sleep for several long minutes...but the heat between my thighs that started with Grant's kiss won't go away.

Finally, I get up, trembling in anticipation as much as with nerves, and creep down the hall. His door is ajar. I listen at it for a moment, and then slip inside, closing it quietly behind me.

His bedroom is enormous, dominated by a huge sleigh-frame bed with elaborate carvings and a nest of down comforters. He breathes softly in its embrace, and I move to his side, staring down at his sleeping face. I hope I'm not overstepping myself, but...*maybe he's been waiting for me to make a move this entire time.*

I slip in under the covers and he stirs against me, rolling

toward me with a grunt. Too late, I realize that he's almost completely naked, except for a pair of loose drawstring shorts. The heat of his skin sinks into me through the thin silk of my nightie, and I nestle in beside him, already filling with a drowsy delight at his closeness.

He stays asleep; he must be exhausted. One arm slides limply around me, and he buries his face in my hair. My whole body tingles, and without any real knowledge of how to go about these things, I twine one leg around his thigh and rub my body softly against his side.

This time he lets out a little rumble and pulls me closer, and I feel his cock stir against my belly. It feels enormous—thick, hefty, and quickly going from soft brushes against me to a hard push. My belly flutters, and I feel my cunt tighten with the urge to feel him inside me.

I would never have been this bold with James. But I'm realizing now that James never really did much to attract my attention or my desire. He just got in my face with what he wanted, and expected me to deliver. And I did, for a while.

I don't want to push Grant away, ever. I want to draw closer to him, until his warmth sinks all the way in and drives away the chill from deep in my bones. I want to wake up next to him, not some snoring mouth-breather who drinks himself to sleep every night.

Grant's eyes still haven't stirred. I grow braver, climbing atop him as he lies on his back. I draw the quilts around us as I go, so our skin doesn't get chilled.

I am settling in when his eyes finally open, and he smiles.

I freeze for a moment, feeling a little guilty, but unbelievably turned on as well. The corner of his mouth tugs up, and he licks his lips. "I was hoping you'd come visit."

"Oh," I murmur, swallowing hard as chills and waves of heat running through me in turns. "Good."

His hands grip my hips as I straddle his thighs, and he leans up to kiss me, his cock trapped between us. His grip shifts to my ass and he squeezes gently, then more firmly as I rock back against his hands. We kiss, and this time it starts out tender, but catches fire fast as he pulls me closer.

He's careful with his strength, until his kisses and the slow sweep of his hands over my arms and back leave me trembling and feverish. My shyness is ebbing away as everything outside of these new sensations and emotions starts to fade into the background.

My skin feels like it's on fire even in the light, sleeveless silk. His thick fingertips slide under the delicate straps; he can cup a shoulder in each of his big hands. He could break me, if he wanted—he's far stronger than James ever was. But he's also far gentler.

The combination soothes and arouses me even further. It feels like I'm sinking into a hot bath. His kisses intensify and turn lingering and sensual. He darts his tongue into my mouth even as his fingers run over the silk at the sides of my breasts.

He tastes of mint gum and brandy, and I'm almost disappointed when his kiss trails away from my mouth. But then he starts kissing my neck, and his hands slide around to stroke my breasts through the silk, and I whimper, having to grab his shoulder to keep upright. My head falls back into the cup of his palm and he brings his knees up as he lifts his hips under me.

His cock slides against me through two thin layers of cloth, throbbing and jumping a little with each heartbeat. His hands push the straps of the nightgown off my shoulders and tug the thin sheath of cloth downward. I slip my arms free and shimmy slightly, wiggling out of the confining silk until my breasts bounce free and my nipples tighten in the cool air.

He groans and cups them both, pushing them together and leaning forward to bury his face between them. I cradle him, hands buried in his hair, and whimper as his tongue traces over my skin. His breath blows hot over one of my nipples—and then he runs his tongue over it and I almost squirm away from the intensity.

He grips me harder and I struggle a little on reflex as he suckles firmly at my breast in long, slow pulls, filling me with greater pleasure than I have ever experienced. I squirm and whimper as my mind and body try to figure out what to do with all this sensation.

I bite back the urge to moan aloud as he seizes the other nipple with his mouth and sucks it roughly. I whimper, and my body goes rigid and slowly grinds against him. He chuckles against my skin...and then one of his hands lets go of my breast and slips under the nightgown puddled on the tops of my thighs.

I feel his fingertips slide over the outer lips of my cunt and gasp aloud as he starts exploring me. Just the outside at first, stroking softly, before firmly kneading in time to his suckling. The doubled sensation makes it almost impossible to cry out— I'm panting so heavily I can't get my breath.

I rock back and forth on his hard thighs as he kneads and strokes my pussy, then dips his fingers into my aching slit and starts to stroke them up and down. I squirm and he focuses in more and more on my clit, circling two fingertips over it carefully, then more firmly.

I pant, my breath so harsh it burns my throat, but the rest of my body is so feverish with pleasure that even the pain is laced with it. "Oh, oh, oh..." I gasp, feeling my body start to shake uncontrollably, and even the soft vocalizations feel good as they leave my throat.

I want to scream. My head falls back—and his big hand covers my mouth. I whimper through his fingers, mixed with desperate, muffled pleas begging him not to stop.

My hips pump against his thighs as he strokes my clit. I feel him slide down underneath me so that I'm grinding against the thick, hot shaft of his cock, now freed from his briefs. I hear him groan, even as the urge to scream grows in my throat along with the pressure mounting between my hips.

My back arches, my thighs strain, and I lift up on my knees—and he guides me, curling his hips under me to settle me onto his cock inch by inch. He's thick, stretching me, intensifying the sensations as he goes back to pleasuring me.

His attention makes me squirm rhythmically, faster and faster, dancing over and around his cock while he grunts and bucks his head back, a strained look growing on his face. "Yeah! Yeah..." he pants, and starts raising his hips to meet mine.

He sinks deep, filling me as his fingers work their magic—and then he tightens his hand over my mouth again as I explode around him.

My body goes wild, muscles rippling around his shaft as I wail against his hand. It's so *good,* and I squirm wildly against him as spasm after spasm rolls through my body, bringing ecstasy and then deep relief.

When my mind is my own again I look down to see Grant stretched under me, sweat gleaming on his skin, every muscle taut as his hips roll reflexively. Fascinated, I force my tired hips to roll against him, milking his trembling cock.

"Oh, yeah, baby. Yeah, just like that...just there...yeah...." he whispers, clutching my hips as his own move sensually under me. It excites me so much to see him like that that my flesh tightens around him again, and I work my hips harder.

His eyes squeeze closed and his lips part as he lets out a primal shout of pleasure—and then I muffle his groans with my mouth. He lifts his hips hard against me and freezes, and I grind against him with everything I have left.

His grip on me is almost painful as his growling cries vibrate in his throat. Inside of me, his cock pulses hard, and then he slowly goes limp. I'm tired, sore, sweaty, but completely relaxed and feeling strangely...triumphant.

Panting, he draws me down to his chest, smiling into my hair. "I love you, sweetheart," he whispers. "I'm not letting you go after this."

"Don't," I murmur against his throat, tears pricking my eyes. "Don't ever let me go."

9

GRANT

I didn't let Emily go. James still can't be persuaded to leave her alone—but since he has not actually been violent we couldn't get her an emergency restraining order, and the regular process was delayed by the holidays. So as a solution, Emily came to stay at my home full time.

She's staying in her own room while we try to figure out what to tell Molly. Emily has moved many of her clothes and her laptop in, though she never actually sleeps in that guest bed except to take naps. She sleeps with me...well, eventually she sleeps.

We ate Thanksgiving dinner together and talked about what we wanted to do for Christmas. Emily looks after Molly while I go to meetings—and when I scramble around looking for a proper Christmas gift for the woman I hope to propose to soon.

I don't want to rush her. But every time I wake up to her face, I know that Emily is my second chance at a real love match, and someone who could love my daughter as much as I do. And she seems so much happier with us—she's even stopped having nightmares.

No thanks to James, though.

I hear him banging on the door downstairs and open an eye, checking my watch. Two fifteen—exactly fifteen minutes after the last bar in Woodstock closes for the night. Emily stirs and I kiss her temple, whispering in her ear, "Shh, I'll take care of it."

James is blocked on Emily's cell phone and her house phone now. We have two of my security guys from the city looking after her house in case that idiot decides to throw another rock through her window. I personally deliver Molly to and from play dates, doctor appointments, and school, and every time that idiot James tries to tail us anywhere I swing right past the police department and he scurries off.

The police are getting as tired of his crap as we are, and every time I call them on him his mother ends up crying on the phone to me about having to bail him out again. I'm losing patience with her as well. Nobody should ever have this big of a blind spot about their offspring. I just pray I can do a lot better by Molly.

I'm in flannel pajama pants with my robe hanging open when I show up downstairs and look out the spyhole. James is out there, eyes bleary, face red and hair mussed. He's forgotten his coat and his breath is misting. He steps forward to bang again—and I open the door and step outside in my slippers, ignoring the chill.

"Get off my porch," I instruct James in a low, cold voice. He stares at me angrily and I see he's drawn a dick in the snow on my SUV windshield. "Leave, James," I sigh—and he spits at me.

I duck aside and it strikes the door, and I take a half-step forward. He scrambles backward away from me, his face screwing up petulantly. "You stole my girl, you piece of shit!"

"Nobody stole anything from you. You drove Emily away and now you're stalking her. I didn't steal her, I'm protecting her. From you." I stare into his eyes—but there's no recognition there. He can't even see that what he's doing is wrong.

"No, no, you're tricking her, and you're keeping her from me." He stabs a finger in my direction, spit spraying from his lips. "And you better give her back before I take away someone of yours!"

I go cold and feel my fists clench hard enough that my knuckles crack. "One, she's a person, not an object, and you're the one who drove her away. Two, if you *ever* threaten me or mine again, the police will be picking you up from the hospital."

He stares back at me defiantly, his chest heaving—and I take another step in his direction. The little coward darts away, leaving me standing there shivering more with anger than with cold.

We don't hear from him again for weeks after that, as the year rolls on toward its close. Christmas decorations go up and we get a live tree like we always do, which we'll plant among its fellows on one side of my yard. I make sure to make the yard ablaze with light from Christmas decorations, leaving as few shadows as possible that James could hide in.

I don't trust his silence, even though it means Emily gets some relief for a while.

It's the first week of December when she belatedly gives me the best idea for a Christmas present. "Would you mind if we visited Cranburg House over Christmas?" she asks softly. "Some of those kids won't get gifts this year."

"We should bring them Christmas too, since you came from there," Molly agrees firmly, and I laugh and nod my concession, outnumbered.

"I'll make some calls," I promise.

Locked in my office, I phone up the director of Cranburg, who is...on vacation. Most of the staff, too. The skeleton crew left includes Marcie, a new caretaker who sounds younger than Emily and a little baffled. It takes her some persuading—

including some compensation for her time—but finally she agrees to make the arrangements.

We all go into a whirlwind of buying and preparing as we grab everything ten kids will need for a good Christmas: food, gifts, a tree, games and all. Their dinner will be on the twenty-second, which is the closest day to Christmas where we can get enough staff to take a shift to help us pull it off.

Late that morning the three of us busy ourselves running back and forth to the SUV, packing it full of everything we need to roll up to Cranburg bringing the party with us. We're about halfway through—the dogs are locked in the basement playroom to keep them from getting underfoot, and I'm lugging a stack of boxes out the door when Emily says suddenly, in a high, nervous voice, "Where's Molly?"

For a moment my train of thought derails and I feel a chill roll down my spine. *She's probably in the bathroom,* I try to tell myself, but I know Emily's instincts for danger are keener than mine. "Molly?" I call out from the porch, at the top of my lungs.

Silence.

My world seems to freeze around me—and then a surge of white-hot adrenaline roars through me, thawing me in an instant. "Molly!"

"Stay here," I order Emily, in case Molly wanders up while I'm running around like a madman. I start looking around everywhere—the house, the yard, the neighbor's yard. Nothing. And slowly, my mind comes to the only conclusion it can: *James.*

His threat rings in my head as I race around the side yard back toward Emily. "It's James, he must have grabbed her," I growl, pulling out my cell to call the police. I then notice she already has hers out. "What are you doing?"

"We didn't hear a car, so he's on foot. It's been under five minutes and I've been watching the street. You would have seen him if he tried to cut through the yard, and both your neighbors have dogs. So he must be hiding with her nearby."

That just angers me more. "Molly!" I call, and listen hard for an answer. *I'm gonna kill this guy.* "Are you calling the cops?"

"No," she says with a grim tone." I'm unblocking James and calling him."

"He can't be stupid enough to not mute his phone—" I start, and then remember who I'm talking about and suddenly feel a bit better about my daughter's odds.

A few seconds later, "Twerk It" blares out loudly from a nearby neighbor's bushes.

I cross the street in about two long steps and dive into the mass of branches. James is there, crouched with his hand over Molly's mouth and staring at me in wide-eyed panic.

"I'll hurt her!" he warns—and then yells in pain as Molly bites his hand. I yank his arm from around her and she bolts out of the bushes, running for Emily with a high-pitched scream. Still holding his arm, I use it to yank him all the way out of the bushes and into the middle of the street.

He sprawls on the blacktop, then scrambles up, looking between me and Emily with growing worry. His jaw sets and he takes a step toward my girls, as if planning to try and take a hostage again.

My fist crashes into the side of his head before he's halfway there. He wobbles completely around, stumbles, pitches forward, and lands in a heap at Emily's feet. He looks up at her blearily—and Molly steps forward and kicks him between the eyes. "Jerk. You smell, too. And you're stupid."

James just lies there, probably playing dead so no one will hit him again. I pull Molly back into a tight hug, and she wiggles a bit before relaxing. She's still more furious than scared, and I'm proud of her, just as I am of Emily.

It's a bad lesson to have to teach Molly; violence doesn't solve anything, unless it's something like a complete idiot trying to kidnap you from your family. Then violence is often what's needed—and deserved.

I just wish she could have been a little older before she had to learn that.

Emily hurries to my side. I grab her with my other arm and hug my girls tight. "Sorry, sweetheart, we're gonna be a little late bringing dinner. I gotta drop this guy off with the cops first."

She nods, sighing tiredly. "That's fine. I know we'll get there."

We get there at seven and order massive amounts of pizza so the kids aren't waiting for us to roast the turkey. There are ten of them—all ages, all kinds, most disabled in one way or another. Some of them can't stop fighting, even during dinner, and eye us suspiciously when we bring gifts.

None of them remember Emily, and the staff has turned over so much that nobody there that night was working there when this was her home. But several of the kids do seem happier for our visit, and that's good. They're going to be seeing a lot of us, soon.

Three days later, I wake up around dawn curled around Emily from behind, and look out the window to see snow falling past the panes in thick, feathery flakes. Molly hasn't stirred yet; I know because as soon as she's fully awake she'll be in here like a shot demanding presents, with two rambunctious dogs on her heels.

I smile and settle back in, burying my nose in Emily's hair. She stirs and rolls over, opening her eyes blearily, and I kiss her on the nose. "Good morning," I murmur.

Emily smiles. "Good morning."

It's been a rough three days. We're pressing charges against James for his kidnapping attempt, but his mother's being a pest about it and will likely hire him a very good lawyer. It will be something of a long haul to get rid of him for good—but that's fine. I'm willing to fight for my new family.

"Mmm," she murmurs as I cup her breast and pull her closer. "How much time do we have before we deal with Christmas morning stuff?"

"Enough, I'm sure," I reply, my cock stirring against her belly as I lean over to kiss her.

As if on cue, from outside my door we hear, "Daaaaad! It's Christmaaaaas!"

Emily bursts into giggles as I back off and grin sheepishly. "Or not."

The End

SIGN UP TO RECEIVE FREE BOOKS

Sign Up to Receive Free E-Books and Audiobook Codes.

Would you like to read **The Unexpected Nanny, Dirty Little Virgin** and **other romance books** for **free**?

You can sign up to receive these free e-books and audiobooks by typing this link into your browser:

https://www.steamyromance.info/free-books-and-audiobooks-hot-and-steamy/

Or this one:

https://www.steamyromance.info/the-unexpected-nanny-free/

PREVIEW OF THE VIRGIN'S TEACHER

An Older Man Younger Woman Romance

By Alisha Star

~

The Virgin's Teacher

His kid is amazing. He gets it from his dad, obviously. And I'm falling dangerously fast for my professor ...

I wasn't looking for anything but a little escape that night, okay?
Not even looking for that, really, but my roommate Annie dragged me out to prevent me from combusting into nunhood.
How was I supposed to know he'd be on the dance floor?
What were the chances that the next day the same Adonis would walk into the class I'd just signed up for?
Not a good idea, Hannah.
But there was no escaping the attraction. My common sense ...
just ... *poof.*

And then he asked me to babysit his kid.
Like I was going to say no to an adorable 7-year-old. Or to the chance to spend time with his dad.
Yes, I know; bad idea all around.
We agreed we were going to keep it totally professional.
That was doable, right?
WRONG.
'Doable' was Austin Parks, along with kind, funny, a great dad, an amazing teacher ...
So how did Mr. Amazing end up breaking my heart into a million smithereens? And can I ever forgive him?

A 7-year-old who needs a babysitter. A 20-something-year-old who set me on fire on the dance floor. And one major problem, namely, when she walked into my classroom the next day ...
What do you do when the first woman to light you up in years turns out to be your student?
Stay as far away as you can, obviously.
But what if she's as amazing as she is beautiful and she's willing to help out with your babysitting situation?
I can totally hire her and keep it on the level.
Just don't get me alone with her, ever ...
We're both adults. Yeah, there's an attraction between us. A major attraction. A flaming elephant in the room that can't be avoided. Except it has to be, right?
Well, matter of fact ...
WRONG!
There is no way I'm letting this one get away. She's the best thing to ever happen to me or my kid. Except that I'm sort of kind of ...

A total jerk.

Yeah, I own it. Can I ever win her back after my colossal screw up, though? I have to. Because my life isn't worth anything without Hannah Cosgrove in it.

CHAPTER ONE

"You need to get out and par-tay!" Annie yelled into my face, breathing her cranberry vodka breath all over me. I rolled my eyes. I always tried to be the voice of reason, but somehow Annie always got her way.

"I need to get some sleep, is what I need," I replied tartly. "I've got an intense semester ahead. Who knows when I'll be able to get another full night's sleep?"

It was Annie's turn to roll her eyes. "Honestly, Hannah, you're ridiculous. Here we are, on the verge of our final semester of college. We've worked so hard and we'll be out in the world before we know it, but you can't even let yourself enjoy it."

"You don't call this enjoying it?" I raised my own cup of booze.

"No, I mean we should go out."

"You know I hate that. I can never enjoy myself."

"You never let yourself! You're such an amazing person. You're allowed to have a little fun in your life, you know? And besides, in a year, you'll probably turn completely to your homebody ways. Let me get at least one more night of fun with you."

She waggled her eyebrows at me. I sighed at her and flipped

my hair over my other shoulder, thinking back. Annie and I had come a long way from the tiny babies we were when we'd first met as college freshmen. I was so awkward then. It didn't help that I had just moved miles from my small hometown in Pennsylvania to the den of wonder and sin that is New York City. I was studying journalism and it felt like everyone in my classes wanted to jump in front of speeding trains and cut their way through thick jungles just to get the best story. All I wanted to do was write about fashion, film, and all the glamorous people living in the glittering city.

Sure, I had fun. And with my work accumulating, there wasn't an internship I wanted that I didn't get. But, looking at it now, I was struck by how lonely those first years had been. Maybe I'd come off as standoffish, or maybe I'd just been too shy, but I hadn't made many friends during those years.

Except Annie, of course. She lived down the hall from me in the dorms. Those nights that I'd be sitting up, writing and researching for hours, Annie would knock on my door with a boisterous smile and a six pack from the bodega around the corner. Just before our junior year we moved out of the dorms and into a tiny two-bedroom apartment. All the while, Annie would drag me to parties and adventures with her parade of friends that she somehow made everywhere she went. Between her red hair and sparkling green eyes, and my brown on blue, we always attracted attention.

"If I show up to class tomorrow hungover, it'll be your fault."

"Yay, senioritis!"

"I'm serious. And so broke! I still need to find a job for this semester."

"Only you would give yourself a completely full course schedule for your last semester and also try to take a job while doing it. Come on. You know you want to ..."

Folding my laptop and putting it aside on my bed, I walked

over to the wing-backed chair next to my window. It was one of the only things I'd splurged on when I'd first moved out of the dorm. Not even my mattress was as comfortable. I liked to sit there and stare out the window at the shining stars and city below. I sighed, my breath slightly fogging the window for a second.

"Honey, you need a man," she informed me, not for the first time. Annie was moderately obsessed with my love life.

"It's not that I wouldn't like one," I replied. "I just ... it's never right, you know?"

"No, I don't know," she replied. "Did you study journalism or poetry? Because I know about all your big dreams about the perfect romance, but that stuff isn't real. If you want to find someone to hang out or okay, fine, fine, to spend your *life* with, you have to go through a few duds first."

I shrugged. "Maybe it sounds silly ... but I can't help what I want. Sparks and all."

"You're picky. I get it." Annie got up and held my hands in hers. For all her teasing, I knew that she cared about me and wanted the best for me. "No random one-night hookups, then. But we still deserve a party. Why not go out there and make them want us a little bit?"

I smiled and looked back out at the city. New York had always symbolized a new beginning to me; a world of endless possibilities. And maybe Annie was right. Maybe I had been so focused on my studies that I'd hardly made any room for life and passion. Who knew where I'd be in a year? Maybe, at least a little bit, I could grab the world by the horns while I still had a chance.

"I don't know how, but you've convinced me to have yet another night of debauchery," I said.

"Hurray to bad influences!" Annie cheered. "Now, finish your drink so I can do your makeup. We're going to do the night right."

CHAPTER TWO

The club was abnormally crowded for a Sunday night. Apparently we weren't the only ones looking to have a final hurrah before the semester started. The dance floor was absolutely packed. Go-go dancers danced as the DJ mixed his tracks on the stage above, surrounded by an all-chrome turntable. The crowd and smell of sweat reminded me why I usually avoided clubs like this at all costs. But the music was thumping and I was feeling the drinks from earlier as I danced with Annie.

A small but dynamic man approached us with two drinks and a huge smile. He made eye contact with my breasts before he did with my eyes. I could already feel the eye roll coming on. And the creeps, I thought. I didn't come to clubs much, and one big reason was the creeps. They lived in the walls, apparently.

"Good evening, ladies," the stranger rumbled. "Hope you're having a fun time."

"The best!" Annie responded, throwing him her most charming smile.

"The drinks are compliments of my friend over there," he continued, gesturing to a man leaning against the bar, who raised his own drink at us. "He was wondering if you'd like to join us at the bar."

Annie turned to me and raised her eyebrows. "Would we?"

I shook my head. "You two go right on ahead. I'm enjoying myself here."

A flash of concern and sincerity crossed her face. "Seriously?"

I nodded, genuinely wanting her to enjoy herself too. "Sure, have fun! I am."

Annie nodded before threading her arm through the stranger's and walking up toward the glowing wall of liquor at the bar. I continued dancing, lost in my own bliss and enjoyment of the moment. I spend my life planning for things and thinking about the future. I like to seize moments like this, when I am completely and purely living in the now. I let the music flow through me and the rest of the club patrons drifted away. I didn't think about how much my feet were killing me in those heels or what I looked like to other people. It was so freeing. In a way, I was happy Annie wasn't even with me in that moment. I was able to have some pure, alcohol-fueled fun, away from the sight of anyone who knew me.

I was nodding my head back and forth to the music when I opened my eyes and saw him.

There was a man dancing a few yards away from me. The first thing I noticed was he was absolutely stunning. He was wearing a dark button-down shirt, which pulled slightly over his strong arms and broad shoulders. I had never before seen someone wear jeans so well, and as he moved his hips, I couldn't draw my eyes away from his round, perfectly sized ass. His skin seemed to glisten and change colors in time with the beat and flashing lights on the dance floor. He had medium-length blonde hair with a slight curl to it; the roots dark with his sweat.

His clean-shaven, square jaw framed out one of the most handsome faces I'd ever seen.

He was also dancing alone. I wondered who he'd come here with.

And just as I was about to look away and blush at the thought of ogling a complete stranger, he looked up and we made eye contact. His eyes were crystalline blue, like a clear, open sky or the perfect Caribbean water. I swallowed hard. For some reason, I felt the sudden need to chug a gallon of water or find the ripest apple in a bunch and sharply bite into it, letting the juice run down my chin. He smiled at me as his eyes watched my throat move.

And then he was moving through the crowd toward me, and I could swear that each one of his footsteps was in time with the frantic beating of my heart.

I was expecting the usual kind of treatment that I got from men in clubs: a gruff grab by the hips, a whisper in my ear promising more, an indelicate dance designed to fuck me through my clothes. Instead, he reached out and gingerly took my hand in his as if it were made of precious porcelain, then gently pressed his lips to the back of my palm. I wanted to laugh. What am I, a princess? But I couldn't bring myself to. The gesture itself was corny, but somehow extremely touching. Very few men in this world could make you feel like an absolute queen in the middle of a sweaty club ...

He looked up. "What's your name?" he said in a dark baritone.

"I'm Hannah," I managed.

"Hannah," he repeated. I felt my whole body clench in anticipation when he said my name. I'd never heard anything like it before. "My name is Austin," he replied.

"Hey," I said inarticulately.

"Mind if I ask you to dance with me? I saw you from across

the room, and I ... well, I absolutely had to try to at least meet you," he said, with a surprising level of sincerity.

"Of course," I said, sliding my hands over his shoulders. Dancing was good. Dancing, I was comfortable with. Dancing, I could handle.

Except I'd never danced with Austin before. The beat thumped through my chest and into his. He was an amazing dancer and he made me feel like we were sharing the same breath. His hands slid up my arms and his fingers slowly glided over my collarbone. He traced thin lines down my sides to my hips, where his hands burned prints into my skin through my form-fitting dress. I could feel my whole body leaning into his, and I thought he might even have been supporting my whole weight in his hands. I was usually a bit of a clumsy dancer in couple's dances, but somehow my feet knew exactly where to go. Dancing with Austin felt incredible and natural. Before I knew it, the song was over.

I was about to mourn the loss of his touch when he leaned in and whispered into my ear.

"Stay with me for the next song?" he murmured.

"Yes." The response came out of me like a sigh. What was it about him? He drew my desire out like poison from a wound.

"Good," he whispered as he drew me closer. "Because I'm not even close to being done with you."

As the deep bass of the next song began, Austin drew me against him, our hips flush and our knees rubbing together as we swayed. This was too intimate... which simultaneously thrilled me and terrified me. This was something I was not comfortable with ... but I couldn't stop.

And then I felt it. I felt his cock pressed up against me through the leg of his pants. I gasped at the contact, but I didn't feel ashamed or shy by it. I moved my leg against him experimentally, and I felt more than heard him moan against me. I pressed my face against his shoulder to hide my blushing. He took it a step further when his hands slid down my back and landed on my ass. He massaged me lightly for a moment, in wide, flat-palmed circles, but then he gripped me, roughly pressing and kneading me, guiding my hips up and down the shape of his cock, positioning himself directly up against the already soaked front part of my panties.

I'm going to cum like this, I realized. I was so turned on, so ready to go, and I could feel him beginning to pick up the pace, getting me closer and closer and ... then he stopped. I was sure he heard my groan of frustration. I pulled slightly away, flushed and flustered, to glare up at him for teasing me. He chuckled in response.

I was so worked up, I barely noticed when he withdrew one of his hands and lifted it to my face. With a finger, he traced my jawline and drew my eyes up to his. I could see the kiss coming from a mile away. His eyes filled with dilated, aroused pupils as he leaned in, waiting for me to stop him. "Trust me, I want to make you fall apart tonight," he breathed against my face. "But I won't do that until I've done this first."

I didn't stop him. From the first moment his lips brushed mine, the kiss exploded. His lips were soft, testing the waters, but skilled and purposeful. Mine were more than happy to follow his lead. Our hands were all over the place, roving over our bodies, and our mouths danced, unaware of the music or the people around us. I moved my hands over his arms, feeling the warm muscles twitch underneath my fingers. I caressed my way down his chest to feel his pecs – his nipples small and hard through his shirt – and made my way down what was clearly a tight, toned stomach. Then he pulled away and whispered in my ear again.

"Come home with me."

Like a glass window, it felt like the world around me shattered. The words were a bucket of cold water to my ecstasy. I jumped back from him as if he were on fire, eyes wide. He held my hands, concern in his eyes.

"Hey. You don't have to if you don't want to. I was just asking."

He reached forward and pushed a strand of hair behind my ear. It was a surprisingly tender gesture for the middle of a dance floor, and I found myself leaning my face into his palm. I kissed the tips of his fingers, lightly biting down on his thumb.

"Hannah!"

I whipped my head toward the sound of my name, and Austin snapped his hand away. It was Annie, waving at me from the other side of the dance floor with her arm wrapped around the man from the bar. God, I'd almost completely forgotten that I was out with her.

"Come on!" she screamed. "These guys know the best place to get a burger nearby!"

I turned back to Austin. He looked strangely downcast, as if he wasn't going to go find a new person to dance with the minute I left. The thought made me feel strangely sad too.

"I should go," I murmured.

"Can I at least get your number?" he asked.

I bit my lip. "Got a pen?"

He pulled a red marker out of the back pocket of his pants. At my raised eyebrow, he chuckled. "I carry these everywhere I go. Weird, I know."

He pulled back his sleeve to show me the pale inside of his lean arm and handed me the marker. I wrote down my number as legibly as possible and handed the marker back. He held my hand and the marker for a moment, stroking the top of my hand with his thumb. I exhaled and looked up. His eyes held the promise of everything he wasn't able to do to me tonight. Finally, he released my hand. He smiled, winked at me, and disappeared, swallowed by the throng of dancing bodies.

I WAS GETTING ready for bed and chugging a massive water when Annie came back into my room.

"So, are you going to tell me about tall, blond, and dance-y yet?"

I rolled my eyes. "I'm just trying to get into bed here."

"You two looked very cozy ..." she teased. "I hope you got his number or something. Things looked positively electric between the two of you."

"I gave him mine." I smiled at her, raising my eyebrows.

"Good. Goodnight, honey!"

She floated out the doorway the same way she came. When I was finally in bed with the lights turned off, my phone lightly buzzed. I opened it up to a text from an unknown number.

I'm sorry our time together was cut short. It was amazing meeting you tonight. -- Austin

I fell asleep with a smile on my face.

THE SMILE DIDN'T LAST. I felt like the dead the next morning. It was a beautiful, crisp winter morning, but I found myself completely unable to enjoy it. I could barely stand being in line for coffee. I checked my watch. Ten minutes until class was supposed to start ... I was cutting it close. The only saving grace of that morning was Austin and I had been texting nonstop.

I could tell he was not looking to play games with me. He was a guy who knew what he wanted. The texts were definitely flirty, but nothing too racy or overt. I preferred it that way. I was a writer. I did like a little bit of innuendo. Plus, things had already gotten so steamy between us on the dance floor the previous night. I was re-reading our most recent text exchange when the roar of the barista raised over the crowd.

"Hannah!"

I jumped, and my headache wailed in response. I glared at the hapless sophomore holding my coffee and snatched it up from him. I half walked, half jogged to the lecture hall, terrified the professor would beat me there. I arrived in a mostly full, professor-less room and sighed in relief. Taking a big, relieved swig of my coffee, I found an empty seat in the middle of the room. I opened my notebook and started to draw some flowers in the corner of the page. I couldn't help that I had to doodle on every piece of paper I saw. I checked my watch again. Even my professor was five minutes late. I went back to my doodling. Eventually, I could hear the door of the lecture hall swing open and a hush fell over the room. Biting my lip, I didn't look up, but concentrated on a leaf shape I was shading in. My ears rang when a familiar voice floated across the room.

"Sorry I'm late. Long night. It looks like many of you had the same."

A small laugh floated around the room. My knuckles turned white as I gripped my pen. No ...it couldn't be.

"Let's jump into it. My name is Dr. Parks and I'll be your professor for Victorian-Era Poetry and Literature. But since we're trying to get to know each other, you can call me Austin."

My head snapped up, and there he was, leaning against the desk at the head of the lecture hall in a flattering button-down shirt, not unlike the one he'd been wearing the night before. His blonde curls were under slightly better control, though, and his hair looked lighter than ever in the daytime. He shuffled a few papers on his podium and pulled a red marker out of his back pocket to mark them up. He cleared his throat and looked up. There was absolutely no mistaking him as his clear blue eyes locked onto mine.

CHAPTER THREE

Standing just inside the door with it locked behind me, her face played in front of my eyes as though my mind was making up for my refusal to look at her throughout the class.

Hannah Cosgrove.

I knew her full name now from the class roster. God, she'd driven me insane when we'd danced together in the club. She'd seemed so confident, so uncaring of anyone else's concerns as she danced alone. But there was something gorgeously pure about her, like fresh, uncut grass or a smooth beach, unmarred by footprints. Beautiful and untouchable. I had to make her mine. I couldn't tell if I had offended her or shocked her when I'd invited her back to my place. And then she'd had to leave with her friend. This was not my first time around the block, but I couldn't help the small voice that was urging me on, insisting that it had never felt like this before.

I'd come to work that morning feeling hungry and hungover, so I'd had to do a double take when I'd seen her sitting almost directly in front of me, looking just as shocked as I felt.

She was my student, of course.

I couldn't get involved now, no matter how much I wanted to. And, God, did I want to. She was gorgeous, magnetic, and absolutely enticing. But it was also too great a conflict of interest. It would put us both at risk. So I was going to have to avoid her at all costs.

She also deserved better than someone who had as much baggage as I did. Danny, my son ... I could never think of him as baggage, of course not. I loved him. I tried to be as good a dad as I could be, given the circumstances. My ex-girlfriend, Vanessa, got pregnant shortly after we graduated high school. I had already left for college, and she'd kept the pregnancy from me for several months. Needless to say, the relationship hadn't lasted long. But Danny had been born on Valentine's Day the next year, and from then on, he had been my world.

He split his time between Vanessa and me, staying with her when I was at school and staying with me while she was working. Vanessa had gotten a job at the local news broadcasting company and worked her way up to being one of the regional correspondents. Meanwhile, I'd worked shit jobs, bussing tables and slinging coffee while I earned my B.A., M.A., and Ph.D. I'd finally gotten to the point where I could do what I wanted to do the most: teach. It was hard for me to believe that Danny was nearly eight now.

I loved Danny and wouldn't trade him for the world. I made some stupid decisions when I was young; some of which I deeply regretted. But I didn't regret him. But I also couldn't ask a student of mine to violate the university rules, be with me, and take on a single dad with a seven-year-old. I knew that no one wanted to deal with that at her age.

But I was still so keyed up from seeing her ... so shocked, so revolted at myself, so ... turned on. The mere sight of her did things to me. My fear of being cornered by her after class dissolved swiftly into desire. I had to struggle all the way through my first lecture, simultaneously trying to do my job and resisting the urge to pull her out of her seat and kiss her like last night.

I sat at my desk for a moment, running my hands through my hair over and over again before eventually relenting and picking up my phone, dialing Leo's extension. It rang twice before he answered.

"Humanities department, this is Leo Renuard."

"It's me."

"Austin! Hey! I wanted to call you. I lost you at the club last night. What happened?"

I started bobbing my knee up and down anxiously. "There was this girl ..."

"Ooh! Scandalous!"

"No, shut up. Listen. I came to class this morning and it turns out she's one of my students."

Leo snorted. "So what?"

"So what?" I repeated in disbelief. "She's my student. Hello? Ethics?"

I could hear him rolling his eyes. "They're in college, Austin. They're adults. We run into them around the city. It's not like you knew she was a student when you were on the dance floor. It happens."

"It doesn't happen to me!"

"With your track record, that's hard to believe."

"She's just ... she's so different." I groaned. "What do I do, man? I can't teach like this. I can't get her out of my mind."

"Listen. You're imagining this person you wanted once on the dance floor. And she's so perfect. She's so sexy that you can't believe how much you want her. But once you realize how young she is, how she's just a person at school, you'll move on. Just try to view her through that mentality. She's just a kid, Austin. A legal kid, but nonetheless. Ultimately, young and naïve and not nearly as interesting as someone your own age with some kind of life experience."

"When you put it that way ..." I sighed. "You're right, you're right."

"She's just a girl, Aussie."

"I know. And my name is Austin."

"Let me live. I'm trying new things over here. Want to get lunch?"

CHAPTER FOUR

"What do you mean I can't drop the class?" I paced the room. Annie pretended not to laugh, sitting in my chair by the window. I gave her a warning look.

"Well, I have to get out of it somehow. There must be another ... okay. Okay, fine. Fine!" I angrily hung up and flung my phone across the room. I flopped down onto my bed, burying my face in the pillow.

"So?"

I turned my face. "I need the credit to graduate on time and all the other classes that satisfy it are completely full."

"Oh, boo hoo, you have to stay in class with Professor McHottyface."

"I'm so glad you find this hilarious."

"Hey," Annie got on the bed next to me. "It's like I was saying the other day. It's your last semester. Maybe now's the time to really go for it, you know?"

"I don't, actually. Go for what?"

"You know what. He's hot and he's clearly into you. Why the heck not?"

"He's my professor."

"He's also a red-blooded man who has needs. And you have needs too! Even if you like to pretend that you don't."

She patted my back. I snorted. It reminded me of my grandmother.

"I have a lunch date so I have to go. You know, though, Hannah ... just think about it."

I didn't acknowledge when she left. I simply waited to hear the sound of my door click closed. I rolled onto my back, staring at the ceiling. I found myself wondering about what Annie had said. I had played it so safe all through college, and now that I thought about it, all through life. Maybe it was time for me to really go there. Whatever I chose, he was stuck being my professor. I had to just deal with it. And, unfortunately, dealing had to happen soon, because as it turned out I had his class in like ... five minutes.

"Shit!" I bolted out of bed as I saw the time, grabbed my books and booked it out of the dorm at top speed.

Turned out class with Austin flew by. He was a really great teacher, and I could say that even though half the time I was listening with one ear while simultaneously watching Austin's mouth as he read aloud. He was wearing his glasses again. Damn those things. I didn't notice he needed them at all until he put them up on his nose to read to us from a book. I found it simultaneously adorable and endearing. He pushed them up his nose and licked his lips as he turned the page. And that made me remember his taste ...

"I remember, I remember," he recited, cutting into my thoughts but not making things better as he recited poetry in that gorgeous voice. "The fir trees dark and high; / I used to think their slender tops / Were close against the sky: / It was a childish ignorance, / But now 'tis little joy. / To know that I am farther off from heav'n / Than when I was a little boy." As he closed the book, you could almost hear the audible sigh from all the women in the lecture hall. He looked up at us and smiled.

"Who can tell me what they think Mr. Hood is referring to when he writes this poem? Simple nostalgia? Or possibly something more?"

The lecture hall was silent. "Really, nothing? I was hoping I would get at least a little more than that," he suggested with a wiggle of his eyebrows.

A giggle passed over the room. He checked his watch. "We're five minutes over anyway. Go home and think on it. If we have silence again on Thursday, I'll start calling people out and I know how you guys feel about that."

What? Time to go already? I stared at the clock in shock.

A nervous chatter. Students began packing up and filing out of the room. I rushed to collect all my things. But just as I was hastening toward the door, I heard my name.

"Hannah."

I stopped hard in my tracks. I turned painfully slow toward him. I had completely forgotten the effect of hearing him speak my name. My knees were already shaking.

"Could you hold on for a second?"

"Y-yes," I stuttered, and he smiled and moved to address a few students who had questions.

When the room had finally emptied completely, Austin turned towards me, and just like that, the electrical connection re-awoke. I could nearly hear it humming in the air. I braced myself for what would happen next, and was surprised when he finally spoke.

"I think there's another class coming in here. Would you mind walking with me to my office?"

The words were so casual, so innocuous, so … innocent, that I actually laughed in response. He smirked at me and rolled his eyes to himself. I could tell we were at least on the same page about how awkward it was to be discussing office hours with someone who had had their tongue down your throat barely a week ago.

"Yes, sure," I finally responded.

"Great. Follow me."

We walked in silence across the campus. I tried to distract myself by observing the world around me, musing at the campus being part city, part college campus, and reflecting on the times I had had in this spot or the other. I still couldn't believe I was only a couple of months away from it all being over. I did this only to ignore the voice in my head urging me to grasp his hand in mine, pull him in, and restart our kiss from the nightclub.

We reached the academic building and didn't stop until we were inside his modest, private office. It was a very tasteful, yet masculine, setup. The walls were absolutely covered in yards and yards of books. His desk was a deep-colored wood with a rich, comfortable-looking leather chair right behind it. In front of the desk sat two inviting chairs facing the window behind it. He didn't seem to have a computer, until I noticed the laptop folded discretely on the corner of the desk.

"You can sit down," he murmured, and I wondered for an alarming second whether or not he could read my mind. I nodded and sat down, crossing my legs and folding my hands in my lap. Austin rounded the desk and sat down, leaning forward immediately.

"Let's just address the elephant in the room, because I know that it's making us both uncomfortable," he began. My mouth felt suddenly very dry. "We met for the first time at a club and ... we did more than just dance."

I would have been surprised if the blush didn't reach my toes. My silence apparently prompted him to continue to speak. "Now, I think that at this stage, there's no point in denying the fact that I'm attracted to you. You've even felt the evidence of that." This remark elicited an audible gasp from me.

Austin chuckled darkly. "But, obviously, our positions as student and teacher in an academic setting must take precedent and I can't act on these feelings." I nodded much more than I had to. I was strangely disappointed to hear this. I knew the rules. I was not sure what I expected. Maybe I had had a small glimmer of hope that now would be the moment we both decided to break the rules. I think more than anything, I was trying to nod through my nervousness. Austin let out a nervous laugh of his own.

"You're allowed to talk too, you know," he commented.

"Sorry," I blurted out. "I'm ... sorry. This is just too weird."

"I agree," he continued. "I just wanted to clear the air. I want you to feel comfortable in class and know that I'm there to be your teacher. I don't want you to think that you can't talk to me or think that you need to avoid me because we had an ... encounter before we knew who the other was." He swallowed harshly. "And I'm sorry if anything I did the other night upset or offended you. I think I got a little demanding, carried away, and I'm sorry for all that."

My eyes widened. This was a different approach. I wasn't expecting this. But I wouldn't forgive myself if I let him continue to think that I was upset by his actions. "Don't apologize for that, please. I actually ... I liked it. I liked it a lot." I could feel myself blushing again at my inability to piece together my words. I looked up to see his eyes darken. He made a low sound in the back of his throat. Had he just growled?

"Don't say that to me. You're not allowed to say things like that to me," he said, barely above a whisper. A beat passed between us where I was sure we would say damn it all to the rules and he'd drag me into his arms, when the phone suddenly shattered the moment. We both jumped at the sound. He cleared his throat, loosened his tie, and picked up the phone.

"Hello? Oh ... he's here now? Yes, of course. Don't leave him standing out there. Let him in."

He hung up the phone and I looked up at him curiously. "Should I go?"

"Only if you want to. Please don't leave on my account. But we will have a visitor: my son, Danny."

"Oh," I said. My eyes instinctively went to check his wedding band ring finger for probably the hundredth time and I saw the same thing as always. It was a bare-naked finger. The thought made me blush a moment as I considered what a "bare-naked Austin" might look like, but the thought was gone as fast as it came. My boldness made Austin laugh uncomfortably.

"Yes, you're correct. No wife."

"Divorced?"

"Not exactly. We were young."

We barely had a moment for the awkwardness of the situation to sink in before his office door burst open on a flurry of blond hair and childhood enthusiasm.

"Dad!"

"Hiya, peanut!" I watched as Austin scooped up his son into his arms for a massive bear hug that the kid seemed to enjoy for a second before realizing he was 'too cool' and scrambling down. Chuckling, Austin ruffled the boy's hair. "I missed you, bug. Bug, meet Hannah. Hannah, this is my son, Danny."

"Hi, Hannah!" Danny said, flashing me a smile devastating enough to rival his father's.

"Hi, Danny. Nice to meet you. How old are you?"

"I'm turning eight!"

"Wow. Congratulations!"

"Thanks."

"What grade are you in school?"

"Second. I get all A's in math," he informed me. "And I like trucks and planes."

"Sounds like we've got a little engineer here."

"That's what my dad always says." He rolled his eyes so endearingly that I grinned.

"Give me just a sec, Danny," Austin said. "Hannah's one of my students. We're just here for a quick meeting." He turned to me. "I'm sorry about this. His mother and I both work, and I still need to hire a sitter for the new semester."

My ears pricked at that. "A sitter? I could do that."

Something unreadable flinched in his face. "Really?"

Hannah, what are you doing?

"Yeah. I mean, I need a job," I blurted, before the voice of reason that had always held me back before could take over now. "And you'll have to find someone to watch him when we're both in class but ... otherwise, I can help out whenever you need." I ignored that insistent voice that warned this was the worst idea ever. In place of that voice, I heard Annie. *Take a chance, Hannah. Just for once in your life, don't play it safe.*

He studied me. "You're sure you'd be all right with that? I could really use the help. If you're uncomfortable, please don't say yes just to be nice."

With one final shove, I kicked my usual caution to the curb. "It's no trouble at all. I'd love to do it."

His smile lit up his cozy office. "Well, great. I'm glad to hear it. So ... how about we do a playdate with you two tomorrow so you can meet and we can see if you're a good fit?"

I nodded enthusiastically. "Sounds perfect. What do you think, Danny? Do you want to go on a playdate with me?"

"Do you like cars?" he asked with comical uncertainty. I was, after all, a girl.

"I don't know much about them, but you can teach me," I replied.

"I can try," Danny agreed, and I bit back a smile at his solemn tone.

Austin cleared his throat. "And in regards to the meeting, you're sure you're okay with this? With me being your professor? We're all good?"

I returned the grin. "Peachy keen."

AS IT TURNED out I had his class in like ... five minutes.

"Shit!" I bolted out of bed as I saw the time, grabbed my books and booked it out of the dorm at top speed.

CHAPTER FIVE

I downed my third whiskey sour before finally saying it out loud. "She's going to be babysitting my kid starting tomorrow."

Leo looked up from his own drink. "Who?"

"Hannah."

"Hannah ...?"

"My student," I reminded him.

"Ah." He cracked his knuckles. "Not quite the approach I suggested you take, I don't think."

I rubbed my temples and flagged down the bartender for another drink. "I tried to. I swear. Every minute I spend with her just makes me want her more. Tomorrow is the test run, but she met him when he came to my office today. I know she'll do great. He's already taken with her."

He gave me a look. "Sounds like he's not the only one."

I glared at him as I got my new drink and immediately downed half of it. "That's not funny."

"Take a joke. Meanwhile, you just need to hook up tonight. You know? Forget her, move on. She can't possibly be that amazing."

"Except ..." I chugged more of my drink. "Except, she is."

Leo suddenly slammed his drink against the bar, sloshing beer over the sides. I jumped in surprise. He had a look on his face that I'd never seen before.

"You don't need this drama in your life and you certainly don't need to be falling in love with a student."

"Love?" I sputtered in shock. "Who said anything about love? Why would you bring that up?"

"It doesn't matter if it's love or not. You're too hung up on her. She seems perfectly nice, but you've got a grown-ass life to live."

"I'm not hung up on her. I'm having a brief ... infatuation."

"Alright, then," Leo challenged. "Prove it. Go take that girl home." He pointed at a tall, beautiful, but decidedly not-Hannah woman leaning against the wall on the other side of the bar. I rolled my eyes.

"I can't take any random girl I choose home, Leo. In case you forgot, that's not how anything in life works."

"Sure, you can't. But you can take home someone who's looked at your ass three times already tonight and you've been too busy feeling sorry for yourself to notice."

I looked back over towards the woman on the wall to find that Leo was right. She was still looking at me. She really was beautiful. Long raven hair, quicksilver eyes and a sly, flirty smile. She was older than Hannah. In fact, the two looked a lot alike ... almost like looking into a picture of Hannah in the future. I finished my drink. I could do this. I could be with her tonight. I couldn't deny that I was attracted to her.

I stood up and straightened my shirt, clearing my throat. "Hold my seat," I told Leo as I headed across the dance floor, automatically recreating the moment that Hannah and I had laid eyes on each other. With her body moving to the sound of the music, my body couldn't help but be drawn to hers like a magnet. When we touched, danced, breathed each other's air, I felt higher than any drug could ever make me.

"Are you going to ask me to dance or just stand there with your jaw hanging open, looking like an idiot?"

I shook my head, clearing my thoughts, as I looked up. The gorgeous brunette was standing directly in front of me, giving me a little smirk and a raised eyebrow.

"You don't look like you really think I'm an idiot," I suggested, the suaveness resurfacing in my voice. Her eyes flickered back up to mine, intrigued.

"I'm Marissa," she said.

"Austin," I responded. "Care to join me on the dance floor?"

"I was starting to worry you wouldn't ask."

I gripped her hand and led her to the center of the dance floor. Her hand was small and warm. But not soft like Hannah's ...

I shook my head again. *Give it a rest!* The booze I'd pounded away was really starting to affect me and I was no longer in control of my mind. I pulled Marissa's hips to mine and began to grind against her. She instantly moaned and bent forward and I couldn't help but moan with her. I ran my hands up her back, over her shoulders, up into her hair ... only it wasn't Marissa's perfume I was breathing in. Not Marissa's skin my hands were moving over. To the beat of the music, the name pulsed in my alcohol-stewed brain.

Hannah Hannah Hannah Hannah.

The room began to spin and I pulled back suddenly.

"Are you okay?" Marissa asked in surprise.

"Gotta go to the bathroom," was the only thing I could say as I rushed off the dance floor. My whole head was floating as I pressed into the bar's bathroom. Thank God, it had been cleaned recently and I pulled myself into an empty stall and locked the door behind me. I stared down at the toilet for a second, trying to decide if I was going to throw up or not. Being off the dance floor and in a well-lit room quieted most of my dizziness. I blinked and rubbed my eyes, trying to return myself back to the present.

What the hell was that back there? What was happening to me?

Visions of Hannah, a mixed bag of my own imagination and the small moments and touches we'd shared, filled my mind. The booze swam in my head, floating on a river of sexual frustration. I thought briefly of going back to the dance floor to collect Marissa for a quickie in the bathroom. But I knew that wasn't what I wanted. It was all wrong. The smell, the taste of her, her height, the exact color of her hair. None of it was right. The look Hannah had given me in my office earlier emerged in my mind, lips pressing together nervously, then the warmth in her eyes as Danny raced in.

My morality was fighting a losing battle. Despite the wrongness, awkwardness, and intensity of the situation, I couldn't turn away. I couldn't stop. I couldn't fight it.

Stumbling out of the stall, I slumped over, scrubbing my hands. For good measure, I splashed some water over my face, trying to clear my head.

Why couldn't I get this girl out of my mind? It was inappropriate, uncalled for, and I didn't need this in my life right now. I had come to the bar tonight thinking about the way she was looking at me when she agreed to babysit Danny, thinking about the tension between the two of us, determined to fuck her the next chance I got. But this was clearly something I couldn't shake. I couldn't even fuck anyone else, because I knew I just wanted her. But if I did that and threw caution to the wind just for her, I would risk everything. My job, my ability to support Danny, my reputation that I'd worked so hard for. Was she really worth all of that? Of course not!

I looked up at my reflection and decided that I hated Hannah Cosgrove. I didn't ... not really. But I couldn't afford to feel drawn to her anymore. It was too dangerous, and it made me act too reckless. I had to stay as far away from her as I possibly could.

But tomorrow she would be coming over to see if she was a good fit to be a sitter for my son. Fuck.

CHAPTER SIX

I rang the doorbell and adjusted my skirt, tugging it down with my hands. Annie and I had a twenty-minute conversation about what I should wear as I was trying to leave the apartment. I insisted that I was only going to test out if I was a good fit for this family, but she wanted me to wear something much more alluring. I flat out refused most of the outfits she pulled out for me, but we finally compromised on a long-sleeved shirt and a knee-length pleated skirt. Annie shoved me out the door, saying she'd be heartbroken if I didn't at least "tease Professor McHottyface a little bit."

Now, I was realizing just how short the skirt was. I'd pulled it down about a hundred times on the subway on my way over. I definitely felt out of place on the stoop of this fancy brownstone in some lovely part of Brooklyn. I couldn't remember the last time I'd visited somewhere so nice.

I was counting the panels on the wood door when suddenly it flew open and a disorganized-but-still-devastatingly-adorable Austin emerged. His hair was disheveled and wild around his face and his shirt was unbuttoned, revealing his white undershirt. He blinked, surprised to see me.

"Hannah, hi! Are you early?"

I frowned and checked my watch. "No? I think I'm just on time."

"Oh," Austin glanced at his own watch. "I must have lost track of time. Please, come in."

He ushered me into the apartment and closed the door behind me, hand hovering over the small of my back, but never touching. We paused in an elegant foyer with high ceilings and a small coat closet.

"Sorry I'm so unprepared. If it works out and you have to take care of a child, you'll get exactly what this whole situation is like." He laughed awkwardly.

"It's fine, please don't worry about it," I insisted. "I'm a guest in your home."

"Danny's just about finishing up his breakfast, so I'll show you into the kitchen."

Austin led me through the foyer, past a lovely staircase with a bannister painted white. The color seemed to be the theme of the apartment. White. Clean. Chic. Masculine. We entered a well-lit kitchen at the rear of the house with a large glass door facing a small backyard. The kitchen was clean with brand-new appliances. At an island in the middle of the room sat Danny, eating eggs and sitting on a tall bar-style chair. He was leafing through a comic book and looked up at the sound of us entering the room.

"Hi Hannah!" he said, smiling at me.

"Hey, Danny, ready for our playdate today?"

"Yeah! Dad got me a brand-new car magazine so I can teach you stuff!"

"Not so fast, bud," Austin interjected, and I caught the smile hiding in his eyes. "You've still got to change out of your pajamas, kid."

"Oh, yeah," Danny said, looking down at his Spiderman-themed jammies. "I'll be right back!"

Danny dashed out of the room, leaving his plate behind. I could hear his rushed steps pounding up the staircase. Austin gave me a self-deprecating smile as he picked up Danny's discarded plate and put it in the dishwasher.

"Seems like the teacher's going to become the student today," he said with a grin.

"I love to learn," I replied, then offered, "I can get that for you."

"Please, don't worry."

"I'm sure the breakfast cleanup is definitely part of the job," I reasoned. I walked around the island to take the plate from him, trying to convince myself that I wasn't just doing it to find an excuse to get closer to him. Our fingers brushed as I gripped the plate. Was that a sharp intake of air from him? I glanced up at him from beneath my eyelashes to glimpse his heated look. Smiling to myself in satisfaction, I turned to the sink, rinsing the plate and fork before bending to drop them in the dishwasher.

Closing the dishwasher door, I rose and was surprised to find that Austin was standing apart from me, on the opposite side of the island, as far as he could possibly get while still being in the same room. He had a possessed look on his face, troubled and stormy. I had sensed his dark mood from the moment I stepped in the door, but had to bite my tongue. It was so obvious in his body language, though, that I opened my mouth to say something, to see what could possibly be on his mind.

But I never had the chance. I barely had a word out before the sound of the front door opened and closed, surprising us both. The sound of heels echoed in the foyer.

"Hello? Anybody home?"

"Mom!"

Danny's rushed footsteps barreled down the stairs. Austin

frowned and moved into the foyer with an urgency I was sure I hadn't seen him move with before. I could feel my stomach drop to my feet as I cautiously followed him. In the foyer, Danny was embracing one of the most glamorous women I'd ever seen. She had long, impeccable legs, and was intelligently dressed in a perfectly matching and fitted skirt and top underneath this season's nicest winter coat. Her bone structure was insane. Feminine clavicle bones framed a long, swan-like neck, traveling up into the perfectly shaped-v of her jawline. High, royal-looking cheekbones sat above a pert chin and pouty lips. She had ice-cold blue eyes, deeply set underneath perfectly groomed brows. Flawless pale skin ended at a head of luscious blonde hair pulled back into a stylish knot at the back of her head.

"It's my baby boy! Hi, honey!"

"Mom, stop! I'm not a baby anymore!"

"Vanessa, what are you doing here?" I was alarmed at the tone of Austin's voice. There were equal parts shock and confusion, tinged with a little bit of anger. His crossed arms and frowning face spoke of his discomfort with the situation.

"What, I can't visit my son, say hi to my own flesh and blood?"

"You normally call."

"I had to talk to you about that, actually." Vanessa (as it appeared that was her name) turned suddenly and looked at me, as if noticing me for the first time, though I'd been there since Austin entered. "Oh, hello. Who are you?"

I cleared my throat and tried to put on one of my best smiles. "I'm Hannah Cosgrove. I'm one of Austin's students, and hopefully I'll also be babysitting Danny."

"I'm teaching her about cars!" Danny piped up proudly.

Vanessa's eyes flashed as she turned toward Austin. "First-name basis with the students, Austin? That seems very friendly," she said with a sarcastic and serious tone.

"I definitely don't prefer being called 'Mr. Parks' or 'Dr. Parks' all the time," he grimaced. It looked like every word to her caused him pain.

"I'm sure you don't," she said suggestively.

Who the hell did this woman think she was? Well, she was Danny's mother and Austin's ex ... whatever. But the way she had just come right on in and acted like she was in charge of the place didn't sit well with me. It apparently didn't sit well with Austin either. His face was pulled tight with tension, his eyes flashing from Danny to Vanessa, but tactfully avoiding mine.

"Anyway, I have an announcement," she said in a commanding voice. "I will be moving back to Brooklyn so I can be closer to the apple of my eye." She nuzzled Danny's face.

"Seriously?" Danny's eyes lit up.

"Seriously," Vanessa offered. Danny seemed thrilled, but I struggled to find a single thing that was warm about this woman. Everything was cold, from her voice to her smile.

"Vanessa, could we possibly talk in private?" Austin had asked a question, but it sounded more like a demand.

"What's there to discuss?" she asked. "There's nothing more to say. I'm just moving to be closer to him."

"When I got full custody..."

"Danny, can you go get your car magazine so you can start showing me stuff?" I asked, feeling bad for the kid and wanting to spare him the awkward tension between his parents.

Austin shot me a grateful look as Danny darted out of the room and Vanessa continued.

"I know we agreed that'd be best for Danny. It works best for us. And we agreed that I could continue to visit him and have a relationship with him."

"Yes, but moving ..."

"I won't be moving into the house with you!" She laughed, as if the idea was completely ludicrous. "I'll just be a five-minute walk away."

"You've already found a place?" Austin said skeptically.

"I've just made an offer. Fingers crossed they accept."

Austin chewed his lips. He didn't seem happy with any part of the situation. He looked like he was about to say something else when Danny ran back in, clutching his magazine.

Then Vanessa stepped in, and something like jealousy moved across her face. "Danny, you'll have hours with your babysitter. Why don't you take me upstairs first and show me any new robots you've gotten lately?"

"Cars, Mom," he corrected, but looking pleased at her unexpected interested. "Here, Hannah. You can look at it." He put the magazine on the table and they walked out of the room.

I turned to look at Austin, who seemed lost in thought.

"She seems ... nice," I winced as soon as the words left my mouth. *She seems nice?* That was the best thing I could think to say? I felt better when Austin laughed slightly at the comment, lifting the mood. I felt bolder, and dared to ask the question that had been on my mind the minute I walked through the door.

"Are you and Vanessa ... you know ..."

Austin shook his head. "Not since Danny was born. Though, I'd hope you'd know that. No one trying to get back together with someone would dance the way you and I danced that night."

His mention of that night brought back the tension between us. It stole my breath away and I sharply inhaled, holding a moment before I felt I could release it. Austin clearly felt it too and coughed uncomfortably, casually walking across the foyer, again creating space between us.

. . .

Annie burst out laughing. I rolled my eyes and glared at her over the top of my coffee cup. "It's not that funny," I insisted.

"It has to be. It has to be funny, or else it's just sad," Annie insisted, wiping her eyes. "Of course he has a shitty ex! All the good ones do! Especially the ones with kids. Once you stick your dick in Crazy, there's no coming back from it."

"Do all the good ones also have an ex moving five minutes away to 'be closer to her son?'" I asked bitterly.

"No, but now you're starting to sound like a real bitch."

"I am not! Annie, how could you? You're my best friend."

Annie held her hands up in surrender. "Well, take a minute and think about what's really going on here," she insisted. "Austin has this child with her. Whether that was from a one-night stand or because they were so in love and thought they were going to be together forever doesn't matter and is, frankly, none of your business. They have this whole history together, and you don't know the situation. Is it possible she's trying to get back together with Austin? Sure, it is. Did he seem happy to have her there?"

I waited for a moment to see if the question was rhetorical before quietly responding. "No."

"Okay, well, then, if she is trying to get back with him, she's a bit far off from that goal. But it's also entirely possible that she did just move closer to be with her son, which is also completely valid and is her right. And here you are. You had this amazing night with Austin, but you honestly have no claim on him; you have no idea how he feels; and you're serving as a caretaker to his son. And you're also his student! So, I know you feel concerned, but you're jumping to conclusions. I guess what I'm saying is, chill out with the Vanessa thing and live your damn life."

"And what can I do about Austin? This shit between us ... it's ridiculous at this point."

Annie smirked. "As you know, I agree. Maybe just ask him what the deal is."

"You don't think that would be a little bit inappropriate?"

Annie snorted. "There's a lot about this situation that I wonder whether is appropriate," she snapped back.

"Fair point," I said, taking a sip of my coffee.

"What's your plan for the day?" she asked.

I groaned. I did not want to think about that at all. "I actually have an assignment due in Austin's class. A presentation on Lord Alfred Tennyson. I'm really nervous about it. You know how I get with public speaking."

Our freshman year, Annie had pressured me into trying out for the university's Shakespeare company. And though I loved Shakespeare and knew all my lines, at the audition I completely choked. I stuttered through the monologue and the moment I got off stage, I immediately ran to the bathroom and vomited.

"Oh, yeah, good times," Annie said. "You'll do great, though. It's just a class. And your extremely hot professor."

I rolled my eyes. "Thanks so much for the reminder." I glanced down at my watch. "I should get going."

"Me, too. I have work in a bit. Break a leg out there, Juliet!"

I stuck my tongue out at her as I grabbed my purse and headed out the door.

CHAPTER SEVEN

From the moment I walked into the lecture hall, my heart was racing. About half the class had already filed in, and Austin was there, listing the upcoming presenters on the board. I was number three. Good. Close to the top was good, because then I could get it over with and relax for the rest of the class. The anticipation would be over.

I paused inside the doorway, looking at Austin. He was wearing his glasses again, and looked as amazing as always; ass still filling out his paints, with a red marker sticking out of one of his rear pockets. He turned and noticed me standing there.

"Good morning, Hannah. Ready for today?"

I gulped and gave him my best effort at a smile. "Ready as I'll ever be."

He laughed. "I'm sure you'll do great."

My heart lifted a little. "Really?"

He looked at me, realizing I was serious about my nervousness. "Yes. I really do think you'll be amazing up there."

"Not just because I'm going to be taking care of your kid from now on?" I teased.

After Vanessa had left, the dark cloud that seemed to be hovering over Austin lifted a bit. Of course, the day had gone spectacularly well. While Austin caught up on some emails, Danny spent an earnest 30 minutes trying to explain car parts to me, before giving up. So we went to the park instead and watched Danny as he crawled all over the jungle gym and whooshed back and forth on the swings. We spread out a small picnic blanket and shared some sandwiches.

When Austin ran to the water fountain to refill his water bottle, a passing heavily pregnant woman commented to me, "Cute partner and cute son. You must feel very lucky."

I smiled and didn't correct her. And I thought to myself that I did feel very lucky. I felt lucky for all of it.

"Hello? Hannah?"

I realized I'd zoned out and that Austin had been talking to me. "Oh. Sorry!"

Austin shook his head, smiling. "You don't know your own strengths. Give yourself some credit. I'm sure you'll blow us all away."

I smiled shyly at him before taking my seat. I returned, as always, to my nervous doodling. I tapped my foot all the way through the first two presenters, resisting an old compulsive urge to bite my fingernails. The anxious energy was building up everywhere in my body.

"Hannah Cosgrove."

My heart felt like it was about to beat out of my chest, and I couldn't tell if it was because Austin had spoken my name or my nervousness to stand up in front of everything. I made my way down the stairs to the front of the lecture hall, notes in my arms. I set my books down on the podium and cleared my throat. I took a breath.

"Lord ... Lord Alfred Tennyson..." I glanced up at the room

full of uninterested faces. Some people were on their cellphones. My eyes flicked over to the desk where Austin was sitting with his rubric. He looked at me over the rims of his glasses and smiled at me encouragingly, nodding. I smiled back and took another deep breath.

"Lord Alfred Tennyson is a name I'm sure you're all familiar with, but his work speaks for itself."

And I was off.

It was incredible how at ease I felt delivering my report. The words fell from my lips like melted butter, so easily and simply. And whenever I got nervous, all I had to do was glance over at Austin, and I felt stronger knowing that he was on my side.

"'O love, they die in yon rich sky, / They faint on hill or field or river; / Our echoes roll from soul to soul, / And grow forever and ever, / Blow, bugle, blow, set the wild echoes flying, / And answer, echoes, answer, dying, dying, dying.' Many people would say that this poem is about the action of diminishing returns that comes with new love. But I interpret it as an appreciation of the power of those moments. These echoes reverberate for Tennyson because they're beautiful, even if they're brief. Tennyson knows that love is something to be cherished. Something worth fighting for."

I wrapped up my speech, waiting for something, anything to happen. I looked over at Austin. His heated gaze was enough to steal my breath and it must have shown on my face. He shook his head, schooling his features, and cleared his throat.

"Good job, Ms. Cosgrove. Very good. Mr. Craine?"

His attention was entirely on the next student as he began his report.

IT WAS JUST past twilight when I arrived at Austin's brownstone, a sleeping Danny in my arms. He'd had Boy Scouts after school today, so I'd had to pick him up and make sure he made it home. I had carried him the last block and a half after I caught him falling asleep while we were walking.

The house was locked and dark when I arrived. I was secretly relieved. Things between Austin and I had only been getting worse ... or better. I honestly couldn't tell. But the tension had completely gotten out of hand. After our moment during class, I really did not want to run into him tonight. It was a long day and I didn't have it in me to deal with the awkwardness between us, or his hot and cold treatment of me.

I trudged up the stairs and brought Danny to his room. I woke him up briefly to get him into his pajamas and have him brush his teeth. As soon as I tucked him in, he was completely out. I sighed and watched him sleep for a moment, yawning and fighting sleep myself. I turned off the lights and headed back downstairs.

I went into the kitchen, thinking I'd make myself a mug of coffee for the road. Nothing was worse than falling asleep on the subway. I was just closing the kitchen cabinet when I turned to see Austin standing in the kitchen's doorway. I jumped.

"Jesus Christ, you scared me! I didn't think anyone was home," I scolded him.

He didn't respond to me, just looked me directly in the eye. Was he breathing heavily? The attention made me fidgety.

"I hope you don't mind that I was making myself some coffee to take on the subway," I explained. "I'm feeling very sleepy and—"

I was cut off by Austin, who suddenly moved from the doorway, into the room. In four steps, he was directly in front of me, and he reached forward and joined his mouth with mine.

Well, now I wasn't sleepy at all.

My body responded to his instantly. I kissed him back and moaned, gasping for air between kiss after kiss. He grasped my hips and pressed me up against the counter, moaning when every inch of his body came into contact with mine. He moved his lips to my neck, kissing, sucking, and biting. I craned my head backward to give him more access and even in that moment of passion, my thoughts from earlier bubbled to the surface.

"What about ... What about the rules and ... God, that feels good," I moaned anew when he found a tender spot behind my ear.

"Fuck the rules. I'm done with them. I've been losing my mind trying to stay away from you, but I ..." His lips returned to mine and I whimpered. I couldn't believe how amazing it felt. "I'm going to do to you tonight what I should have done on the night we met. And the day after. And every day up until now that I didn't give us this, for the charade we've been playing."

His hungry hands ran up my arms and over the front of my chest, kneading my breasts roughly over my shirt and leaning down to kiss my shoulders, pulling the material aside for skin to skin contact. This time when I gasped, it was both out of surprise and out of pleasure. I'd never been touched there before. All of this was so new to me. His hands were so practiced and sure. I blushed at the thought. I had to tell him. I didn't want to, but if I didn't, he would find out eventually.

"Wait," I said, pulling away from him, even though every cell in my body was screaming, demanding that he and I be joined at once. The confusion and hurt on his face as he pulled away was evident, despite his best efforts to look open and compassionate. *He thinks I'm going to reject him,* I realized. While I was only worried that he would reject me. "There's something I need to tell you."

"Okay," he said, licking his lips.

I took a deep breath to steel myself. "I'm ... I'm a virgin."

His eyes widened in shock. "Seriously?"

I looked down and crossed my arms self-consciously. Austin sputtered an apology. "Sorry, I ... I didn't mean ... There's nothing wrong with that. I'm just completely shocked. The way you are with me just makes it seem like this wasn't your first time. And you're so beautiful. I know that any young man would want you just as much as I do."

I sighed and stared down at my feet. "I know that's probably a lot of pressure for you, but I thought you deserved to know, because—"

Austin cut me off with a soft kiss. This kiss was different than the others we'd shared. Any other time Austin and I had kissed, it had been an insane collision of passion and fire, an extreme dance that felt on fire. This one was affectionate. It was physical reassurance, understanding, a way to say "I'm here with you." He pulled away and stroked my hair.

"I'm glad you told me," he began. "We're not going to fuck tonight."

I couldn't help the crestfallen look on my face. I wanted him. My body wanted him. I was sure I was already embarrassingly wet. But I shouldn't have been surprised that he didn't want me anymore. I knew the virgin thing might be a turn off. But at my saddened look, Austin chuckled and drew my eyes back up to his with a hand on my chin.

"You deserve an amazing first time. Candles, romance, the whole bit. Hannah, I just had you up against the kitchen counter and I would've taken you right here if you hadn't stopped me."

I bit my lip. "I was considering it."

Austin moaned and pressed his forehead against my shoulder. "God, do you have any idea what you do to me?" A tense beat passed between us. Austin seemed to be thinking of something. "Let me show you how much I want you tonight."

My jaw dropped. "But I thought ... you said ..."

"We're not going to fuck. But I want to ... unwrap you tonight."

I gave him a look for his choice of words. He smirked at me and leaned into my right ear. "Have you ever come so hard and so much that you feel like you've completely left your body?"

I was panting as if I'd run a marathon. All I could do was shake my head no. He began stroking his hands up and down the small of my back. "If you'd be open to it, to letting yourself come undone with me, I would love to have you."

I swallowed hard. This was it. I started nodding my head yes, but made sure I could verbalize, too. "Y-Yes. Please. I want that too."

Before I knew it, Austin had hitched me up in his arms, with my legs wrapped around his waist, and was carrying me towards the door. I squeaked quietly to myself and tightened my legs around him, holding on for dear life. I hardly had to. Austin's body was just as solid as I had imagined. I felt impossibly small and light in his arms. He carried me as if he was just moving a set of sheets between rooms.

As he mounted the stairs with ease, he whispered in my ear. "Danny could sleep through a stampede out his bedroom window." I giggled at the remark. "But we still have to take care with the screaming. We wouldn't want him to worry that anything was wrong."

I smirked at him. "Screaming? You're really hyping this, aren't you? It had better be as good as you say it is, otherwise I think I might be disappointed."

He smiled at me knowingly. "I promise you won't be."

We entered his bedroom. I hadn't snooped around in here yet, so I took a moment to observe my surroundings. There was a queen-sized bed at the center of the far wall, with an impeccable, inviting bedspread; a nightstand to the side with a small lamp; a closet next to the small dresser with a television perched overhead; the door to the master suite's bathroom; and a massive window from the ceiling to the floor, pouring moonlight into the room.

Austin walked me over to bed and laid me down gently, kissing me again. "Can I take your clothes off?"

I nodded nervously. It was one thing to think about it, but Austin asking to disrobe me like we were right out of a story and having him there in person wanting me and lying back on his bed was just too much for me. It was all so intense. Austin began with my top. He slowly peeled off my shirt, taking care to lay it on his dresser and continuing to touch and kiss every new piece of exposed skin. He trailed his hands back up to my bra, a hand covering each breast. He started teasing me through and around the thin lace material. His fingers traced the edges of the cups, dipping just slightly underneath to tease the tender flesh of my breasts.

I was lost to the sensation and I could feel my body moving in time with his circular motions, especially my hips as they ground against his thigh. He used his index fingers to trace my nipples through my bra, working them into tight, tender peaks. I was full-out moaning then, desperately seeking a release that still felt so far away. When he pinched my nipples through my bra, sending a jolt directly to my clit, I cried out and couldn't stand it anymore.

"Austin, take it off," I begged.

He grinned wickedly up at me and in a moment, his hand was unclasping my bra and wicking it away. He exhaled for a moment. "So fucking beautiful," he murmured before his hands came up to cover me again. His palms were intensely warm and arousing. He stroked the skin and worked my nipples with his fingers, but then he leaned down and took one of my peaks into his mouth. My hands flew to the back of his head to grip his hair and keep him there because it felt incredibly good. The variety of sensations were driving me insane. The wet flicks of his tongue, the harsh suction of his mouth, the singe of his teeth brushing me while his other hand massaged the neglected breast. He released me to speak.

"You feel close. Think you could come just like this, baby?"

I was incoherent. "I don't ... Maybe ..."

He dove back down to suck my nipple into his mouth, making me keen. But this time, he slung one of my legs over his shoulder and pressed his hips into me, grinding his hard dick down onto me. I moaned out loud. I couldn't believe how close I was just with some nipple stimulation and the best dry humping I think the world had ever seen.

"I think ... Oh God, Austin ... I'm close. I can't believe it, I'm fucking coming." He sped up his pace, doubling his efforts to finish me and then I came, turning into a puddle underneath him.

"Holy shit," he said. "Holy shit. That's the hottest, most amazing thing I've ever seen. You're so fucking responsive."

The echoes of the final waves of my orgasm had my head spinning. I whined, squirming uncomfortably in my jeans. Austin's hand descended down to the zipper fly. "I want to see what I've done to your pussy."

Despite my still-waning orgasm, the statement made me moan and shiver as Austin pulled my pants and underwear down in one go. Once they were off, Austin took another moment to let his eyes rove over my body and admire me. I realized that this was the first time I'd ever been naked in front of another person. Or at least, in a sexual context, not counting locker rooms. I was expecting to feel self-conscious in the moment. But the look on his face dispelled any doubts I might have had on what he thought of my body. He was still completely clothed, and I was now entirely naked. There was something so erotic and arousing about that. At the back of my mind, I recalled getting a wax recently and I silently thanked myself for that foresight. In fact, I wondered if I had made myself smooth because I was expecting him to take me at any moment.

Austin introduced his hands to me slowly, starting by massaging my legs up to my thighs, then tracing his fingers over the junction between the tops of my thighs and my pelvis, slowly drawing narrower and narrower paths until he was just gently teasing my outer lips. He gently spread me and dragged a single fingertip up the soaking length of me, from my entrance to my clit. My hips jolted off the bed in response, which he quickly corrected by using one of his forearms to pin me to the bed. I thought having another person touching me would be like when I touched myself, but the foreignness of Austin's fingers made the sensation feel five times as potent as I was used to.

"Do you ever touch yourself?"

"How do you like it? Slow and smooth?" He drew his fingers torturously slow over my clit, applying pressure, over and over again. "Or do you like it rough and fast?" He started rubbing my clit in frantic circles. A guttural sound emerged from me that I was sure I'd never made before.

"Both," I croaked.

I could've sworn I felt Austin growl as his attentions to my clit increased. I could feel myself chasing the peak again. So soon was completely unheard of. My body just couldn't get enough of him.

"Do you think about me when you touch yourself?"

I keened again, arching against his arm. I nodded again.

"What do you think about?"

I could feel myself blush at the question. "You," I responded.

"What do I do in your fantasies?"

This was more than new to me. I'd never been in a situation where someone was touching me like this or wanted me to tell them what I wanted sexually. I definitely found Austin's dirty talk very arousing, but I wasn't sure if I could do it, too. My feeble attempts so far had seemed to have the same effect on Austin that his words had on me, but I still felt a little self-conscious about the whole thing. I remembered what he had said earlier: that he wanted to unwrap me and he wanted me to be open with him.

Maybe that's what he was doing; trying to test my comfort zone and let me expose myself to him. I could refuse his encouragements if I wanted to, and I was sure he would respect that, but I didn't want to. There was no reason to feel shy. He was here with me, and I wanted to be here with him. I swallowed thickly.

"You touching me, fucking me with your fingers, and ..." I couldn't help but blush. "And your face between my thighs."

"God, really?" His pupils dilated to three times their size. Before I could respond, he was jumping off the bed and yanking me by my feet until my hips sat at the edge. In one swift motion, he was kneeling before me, like a man doing penance, throwing my knees over his shoulders. He used his hand to spread my lips and took one luxurious lick up the length of me. I cried out sharply, slapping my hand over my mouth to muffle the noise. Austin lifted his head.

"Like that?" he asked.

"Yes! Please, don't stop," I moaned as I grabbed onto his bedsheets for dear life. "I'm so close already."

The heat of his mouth on me was driving me insane, lapping over my clit again and again. My legs were shaking against his ministrations and spots began to develop behind my eyes. As the cherry on top of the sundae, his fingers replaced his tongue on my clit and he leaned down to gently insert his tongue into me, slowly fucking me with his tongue. Like that, the coil that had been winding within me snapped and I was flying. My thighs snapped shut, locking over his head, but he did not relent, stroking my body reassuringly as I came down from my high.

My legs went slack, falling loosely to the side. I thought that he was finally done with me. I lay there, completely spent. But then, Austin gently blew on my pussy, making me shiver, and returning his mouth to me, resumed softly penetrating me with his tongue. I shuddered.

"I can't …" I struggled to get the words out. "I can't again. I'm too sensitive."

"You will," he assured, pulling his face away from me briefly. "And I'm not going to touch your clit at all this time. I want to see how much you can take."

I was about to ask him what he meant by that when he inserted one finger into me and began slowly moving in and out of me. His finger was thicker than mine, but it felt amazing.

"You feel so fucking tight."

He added a second finger and my breath hitched. I could definitely feel I was being stretched now.

"Oh, God …" I moaned.

My enthusiasm spurred him on, and he started going faster and faster. I was riding his fingers with abandon and it felt incredible. But I wasn't quite there. My peak seemed slightly out of reach, no matter how hard he went. Suddenly, I felt him add a third finger.

"Oh, shit!" I yelped. The thickness was a heady sensation, with a twinge of discomfort. But before I could say anything, Austin began hooking his fingers inside of me after each thrust, pressing into a spot that felt like a pleasure button attached to every nerve in my body. I started moaning out of control.

"Hannah … come for me, Hannah," Austin's flushed face murmured to me. "I want to feel you come for me again."

One, two, three thrusts later, I was thrashing my head into the bed, trying desperately to muffle my screams as my whole body shook with earth-shattering explosions. When I finally collapsed, I was panting and sweaty, lolling there blissfully, my body present but my head still stuck somewhere in the clouds. I didn't even notice Austin extricate himself from between my thighs and dress for bed.

The exhaustion from earlier was hitting me and I struggled to open my eyes when I felt him tucking my spent body into his bed. He spooned his body behind mine, holding my limp body and landing soft kisses on my shoulders and at the nape of my neck. I was struck suddenly when I felt him, still hard, pressed up against my ass. I fought sleep as I turned to look at him.

"But ... what about you ..." I was interrupted by a deep yawn. God, three orgasms really took a lot out of a woman. Austin just chuckled to himself.

"Another time. Tonight was just about you." He smoothed my sex-tousled hair back. "I was the first person to do any of those things to you, wasn't I?"

He kissed my lips and I could still slightly taste myself on his tongue. "Hm," he whispered. "That's delicious."

I settled into his arms easily. His cozy warmth lulled me to sleep swiftly. I leaned up one last time to press a kiss over his heart, then completely passed out, falling into a deep and sated sleep.

If you want to continue reading this story, you can get your copy from your favorite vendor by searching for the title:

The Virgin's Teacher

An Older Man Younger Woman Romance

You can also find the e-book version by typing this link in your computer's browser:

HTTPS://WWW.HOTANDSTEAMYROMANCE.COM/PRODUCTS/THE-VIRGIN-S-TEACHER-AN-OLDER-MAN-YOUNGER-WOMAN-ROMANCE

OTHER BOOKS BY THIS AUTHOR

Saving Her Rescuer: A Billionaire & A Virgin Romance

I was just trying to get away from my crazy ex for the weekend when I ended up in a giant pileup on the highway up to Gore Mountain.

https://geni.us/SavingHerRescuer

∼

Sensual Sounds: A Rockstar Ménage

Lust. Lies. Double lives.

The rock and roll industry is full of people who are looking out for themselves and willing to do anything to rise to the top.

https://www.hotandsteamyromance.com/collections/frontpage/products/sensual-sounds-a-rockstar-menage

∼

On the Run: A Secret Baby Romance

Murder. Lies. Fraud. Just another day in the lives of billionaires and women on the run.

https://www.hotandsteamyromance.com/collections/frontpage/products/on-the-run-a-secret-baby-romance

∼

The Dirty Doctor's Touch: A Billionaire Doctor Romance

I am a master. An elitist. I am at the top of my field, and I know what I am doing.

https://www.hotandsteamyromance.com/collections/frontpage/products/the-dirty-doctor-s-touch-a-billionaire-doctor-romance

The Hero She Needs: A Single Daddy Next Door Romance

He's the only man I've ever wanted...

https://www.hotandsteamyromance.com/collections/frontpage/products/the-hero-she-needs-a-single-daddy-next-door-romance

You can find all of my books here:

Hot and Steamy Romance

https://www.hotandsteamyromance.com

COPYRIGHT

©Copyright 2020 by Alisha Star - All rights Reserved

In no way is it legal to reproduce, duplicate, or transmit any part of this document in either electronic means or in printed format. Recording of this publication is strictly prohibited and any storage of this document is not allowed unless with written permission from the publisher. All rights are reserved.

Respective authors own all copyrights not held by the publisher.

www.ingramcontent.com/pod-product-compliance
Lightning Source LLC
LaVergne TN
LVHW011718060526
838200LV00051B/2941